RACE –
Instituted by God or Invented by Man

Gerald Phillip Whitaker

ISBN: 978-1-966477-26-6

Library of Congress Control Number: 2025912031

Dedication

To my wife Cheryl & my son Gerell

To my wife Cheryl & my son Gerell

Table of Contents

About the Author

G. Phillip Whitaker was born in the Bronx, New York, and spent his early childhood in the iconic neighborhood of Harlem in Manhattan. His family later moved to Teaneck, New Jersey, where he spent his formative years. The contrast between his private school education and the diverse community in which he was raised shaped his unique perspective on life.

Gerald earned his graduate degree from Alliance Theological Seminary in Nyack, New Jersey. He went on to spend two decades in the field of Information Technology, working as a corporate trainer. Today, he is a business owner, social entrepreneur, pastor, and avid golfer.

He currently resides in New Jersey with his wife of 42 years, Cheryl, and their son, Gerell.

Introduction

I have set out to dispel a belief system that has enveloped the whole earth for centuries. That is this thing called "RACE." I will not give away the gems of truth that are written in the pages to come. However, I think it is necessary to define things; therefore, level setting is our starting place. My hope is that this will assuage any misgivings about the author or the point of view from which this treatise has been written.

Words and phrases have been used to express certain ideological positions, which have, in turn, shaped political, social, and economic structures. Words shape laws, governments, doctrine, and the principal beliefs of people. But are all words and phrases founded on truth? The author offers some answers in the pages of this book. I view this undertaking as a "Truth Project."

I realize that my work here is iconoclastic. It is the author's contribution to the world, an attempt to demolish the cherished and long-held belief system and institution of "Race."

I offer here a list of words that we have attempted to omit or use substitute words and phrases that are counterintuitive to much of our established nomenclatures across the world. I realize that this may trigger some cognitive dissonance, but take the journey of discovery with me, and it will all be worth it.

Substitute Race with Skin Tone

Substitute God with Yah, Elohim (original Hebrew name vs Greek name God)

Substitute Human and Humanity with Mankind (which quite naturally includes women)

Thank you for your purchase of this book, and may the eyes of our hearts be enlightened.

– G. Phillip Whitaker.

Chapter 1: My Early Years

"Go home, nigger!" This was what was shouted at me while I was walking along the highway one day after football practice. A group of four or five guys, with whom I had just finished football practice, sped by me in their car and shouted it. At that time, I was a student at a predominantly white school in the Northeast part of America—New Jersey. I will not mention the school, as it is not my intention to shame anyone.

I was born in the Bronx, NY. At the time, my family was living in Manhattan, a place affectionately and globally known as Harlem. During the early sixties, Harlem was a vibrant, beautiful community of predominantly African American people. It was the burgeoning of the "Black Middle Class." African Americans were becoming more upwardly mobile. Neighborhoods were actually filled with "neighbors." Everyone looked out for one another, and you could leave your door unlocked in the apartment building. I remember, as a small child, running up and down the stairs, in and out of the apartments of neighboring families. It was a real age of innocence. It was a beautiful time.

Then something happened: drugs. Hard drug use began to take over people's lives, and, subsequently, the neighborhoods of Harlem. The quality of life declined rapidly. No longer could you leave your door open. No longer could children run and play unattended. Sadly, it became a dangerous place to live and a place where you did not want to raise a family if you did not have to. The result was an exodus to the suburbs.

My grandfather, grandmother, mother, her two brothers, my brother, and I (by this time, my dad had left my mom, my brother, and myself) packed up and moved to New Jersey, a suburb 15 minutes across the George Washington Bridge, over the Hudson River. Yet it seemed like a thousand miles. For my readers outside the U.S.: Here in the States, some regions are made up of cities with tall buildings and densely populated areas with large business districts. Located outside the city are more rural areas with many one-family residential homes. These are not densely populated and have far fewer business enterprises; these are known as suburbs.

We moved to NJ (suburbia) when I was five years old. I recall my nursery school and first-grade classmates all being melanated people in Harlem. When we moved to NJ, one of the first things I remember is my mom remarrying. The second thing I recall was being put into a parochial school—a Catholic school. This is the school environment where I would spend the next 12 years.

I learned in an environment where the population was 98% so-called "White" and 2% so-called "Black." At the same time, we lived in a predominantly "Black" neighborhood. So, during the day, I engaged with my "White" friends, and when school was over, I engaged with my "Black" friends.

On my first day in a new school, I was making some jokes with the other kids in the class. "We" were caught giggling at times when our teacher was clearly not amused. This is when it happened: "I" was taken out of the class (not we) and marched to the principal's office for causing a disturbance. At the ripe age of 5, something clicked in my little mind that this was not fair. Why was I singled out when a group of us should have all been sitting in the principal's office? This was my introduction to racial discrimination. Several incidents of this nature would take place during my primary and high school years.

Let's get back to that day after football practice. By this time, I was a sophomore in high school. My parents sent me to an all-boys academy. The student population was 700 boys, out of which there were nine "Blacks." As you might imagine, this was not the first time I was subjected to racially charged incidents, but it was soon to be one of my last among schoolmates. Fortunately, they did not stop doing anything to me, but it let me know beyond a shadow of a doubt that these were not my friends and never would be.

There was one other incident that became a tipping point for me. While riding home on the bus (we lived about 30 minutes driving distance from the school), my new gym bag had moved from under my seat unbeknownst to me. I realized it was missing because I saw one of the seniors (a Hispanic guy who seemed to get along well with the "Whites") take my bag and throw it out the window! To my horror, it felt like I had just received a gut punch. But due to fear, I sat there and acted as if I hadn't seen it. When my stop came, I got up and said, "Where is my bag?" only to be met with sly stares and mocking giggles. I got off the bus and went home dejected.

Upon arriving home, I told my mom and dad what happened. My father immediately said, "Go to the principal and tell him that I want that kid to pay for the gym bag." My father was a no-nonsense man. He was a First Sergeant in the Army for 30 years. So, when he gave us an order, we followed it. The next day, I followed his order. I told the principal who had done it. The principal made him pay for the bag indirectly by having him give the money to the principal, who then gave it to me—$10.00 (the cost of a nice Adidas bag in 1978). It would be nice if that were the end of the story—not quite.

The next day, we all rode the bus together to school. I was met by scowls from the bully who had to pay for his transgression. I rode the bus with all the "White" kids and the two other "Black" kids. No words were spoken on the bus. When we arrived at school, we exited the bus and went into the building. Our bus was one of the first to arrive, so the hallways were empty. We all headed to the cafeteria to wait for the first period to begin.

Once in the cafeteria, I went to my locker. Sure enough, the bully followed me. I was trapped—by myself, with nothing but time and opportunity between me and the bully. He began to approach me. Mind you, I was 5'4" and 120 lbs; he was 5'9" and about 180 lbs—a mismatch indeed. As he moved toward me, two other "Black" seniors, both about 6'0" tall, came around the corner. They literally walked up to me, grabbed me by my collar, and said, "Let's go." They looked at the bully with an ice-cold stare that said, "You're not doing anything to him today." I have never seen such a sheepish look on someone's face as I did on the bully's that day. I escaped with all my body parts intact.

When I got home and told my parents about the day's events, the dominant thought in my mind was, "I'm not going to take this anymore. I'm going to have to fight, but I can't fight all of them." So, I proposed to my parents the most sincere and demanding proposition of my teenage life: "Get me out of that school." To my delight, they agreed and transferred me to another parochial school that was more racially diverse. I got along well with the kids there, of all "races" and cultures. By the way, that is where I met my girlfriend and future wife, Cheryl. (At the time of this writing, we have been married for 42 years.)

It should be obvious by now that I have lived a life that has built in me the capacity to relate to all kinds of people. My upbringing has allowed me to work with and befriend people from different walks of life.

"Racism" is not only a part of the American life experience—it is part of the global experience. Whatever "color" you consider yourself or the nationality you belong to, there will be others from different groups who will pre-judge you and treat you with, at the least, tolerance, and, at the extreme, violence.

I want to make a necessary distinction here: there is a difference between nationalism and "colorism." I will expound on this later.

I have personally experienced "racism" in my young adult years, in my professional corporate life, and as a business owner. I do not wish to recount all the negative experiences I have endured. Instead, I would rather spend time in this book exploring solutions to the ugly stain of so-called "race."

My father's decisive response to the gym bag incident, for example, taught me the importance of standing up for what is right, no matter the cost. My parents also made a conscious effort to raise us without bitterness. One vivid memory stands out: My brother and I were playing in the yard, pretending to be football players, when we started teasing each other with the names "blacky" and "whitey." My father overheard us and immediately corrected us, saying, "We do not use those terms in this family. That is not the way you talk about people." This simple yet profound lesson stayed with me throughout my life.

By navigating two distinct worlds—school with predominantly white peers and home with predominantly Black friends—I developed the ability to connect with people from diverse backgrounds. However, this duality also sharpened my awareness of systemic racism and microaggressions. From separate school entrances for Black and white students to overt discrimination, these experiences solidified my resolve to address racial division and injustice.

As I moved into adulthood, the lessons from my childhood remained with me. I continued to face racism in my professional and personal life, but I refused to let it define me. Instead, I chose to focus on fostering understanding and challenging the false narratives surrounding race. It is my belief that by confronting these issues head-on and finding common ground, we can begin to heal the deep wounds caused by centuries of injustice.

Racism is not only a part of the American experience—it is a global issue. While the specifics may vary from place to place, the underlying prejudices and injustices remain the same. My goal in sharing these experiences is not to dwell on the past but to inspire others to take action. Together, we can create a world where everyone is judged not by the color of their skin, but by the content of their character.

Chapter 2: Beginning to Wonder

About 10 years ago, at about the time of the Gym Incident during my sophomore year in high school, for whatever reason—God knows—I began to consider the issue of race and racism. It occurred to me that if all people had to have an origin somewhere, then at one time, we all had to be the same "color." So, whether you believe in the Judeo-Christian account of creation from the Torah or you believe in evolution, the fact still remains that there was an origin to mankind. I began to accept that this was just the way of the world. Some people have built into the fabric of who they are, and they are certain about people who do not look like themselves. This is true for both "Whites" and "Blacks." Both groups often share a propensity to cling to the cherished institution of race.

Let me be clear: many people of different ethnicities subscribe to the notion of race and racism. I use "White" and "Black" because they invariably demonstrate the most pronounced division in the world and are purported to be the polar opposite of one another.

As I matured, I settled on a mindset that "races" simply do not truly mix. Oh yes, there is tolerance among some. There are interracial marriages and a measure of getting along with one another. However, I found this to be very shallow and superficial in most cases. As people groups, there is not a great deal of abandoning preconceived notions about those from another so-called race. Because this must be true, I began to wonder where in history the concept of race began.

I became a believer in God when I was 19 years old. Until then, my Catholic upbringing had not afforded me a practical, daily prescription to implement my faith. However, my mother began attending a church that taught the Word of God in a practical, livable way that made God seem real, approachable, and personally knowable. My mother invited me to attend church with her on Mother's Day. I obliged, being a dutiful son. I had no idea that I would have the single most impactful day of my life.

When I heard the pastor speak, he made God real and personable. I understood that there was a purpose for my being and that the way I would discover it was to devote my life to Him. My complete story of transformation may be the content of a future book—stay tuned.

Sticking with the subject at hand, I realized that even in church life, people were still segregated. By and large, there were "Black" congregations and "White" congregations. Dr. Martin Luther King Jr. is famously quoted as saying, "Sunday morning at 11:00 is the most segregated time in America." Truer words have rarely been spoken.

Fast forward 30 years to age 50. By this time, I had been living my life as a believer for many years. I had been a student of the Bible all those years. I acquired a master's degree in theology from an accredited seminary, worked for a large church, and started a new church, which I still provide pastoral care for today (2024). During this time, I also enjoyed a 20-year career in the field of information technology. Life was going on as usual until one day, it was like God began to speak to me.

I started to examine the cultural context in which the biblical narrative was actually lived. I know that the thoughts I began to have and the questions I began to ask were inspired by Yahuwah—God. This is the Hebrew name for God. Don't get nervous about the name. I'm speaking about the God of the Torah and Tanach (the law and the prophets), the God of Abraham, Isaac, and Jacob, and the God and Father of our Lord Yeshua—Jesus Christ.

I began to question: If the land regions of Israel, Egypt, Assyria, and Turkey are predominantly "Black" and "Brown" people, then what color were the people in the Bible? Further supplementing this line of thought is the fact that the term "Middle East" is a term of modernity. This landmass and region of the world, prior to colonization, was called Africa—the Land of Ham. And what is the overwhelming color of people from this part of the world? "Black." I had to conclude, from an intellectually honest perspective, that the people I had been reading about all my life in the scriptures were not "White." This thought, inspired by God, changed my understanding of many things concerning faith and practice.

It became clear to me that all humans must have had a common origin, regardless of whether one subscribes to the biblical account or the theory of evolution. If you are someone who subscribes to Darwin's *Origin of Species* or other evolutionary theories, I would argue that even if mankind evolved from some kind of protoplasm under perfect conditions to produce the incredible complexity of the human body (and this sounds weird to me even as I write it), we would still have all come from a particular origin of one. Originally, we would have all been the same color.

Conversely, the creation story in *Bereshit* (Genesis) of the Torah—also known to some as the Bible—states unapologetically that God (Intelligent Design) created mankind and, for that matter, the whole universe. It says God created man in His image and likeness. Referring to Adam and Eve, they would have been the same color, and all their offspring would have been, you guessed it, the same color.

I said to myself, "Self, you are onto something." I set out to discover where in history this use of the color divide began to dominate the thinking of man.

We must reach into history to discover the origins of the use of "Race" in the normal discourse and the personal, daily life-interactions of mankind. Robert Wald Sussman provides quite an astonishing revelation concerning the modern development of Race. In 1775, Johann Friedrich Blumenbach (a German physician) published the first edition of his dissertation, *On the Natural Variety of Mankind,* in which he stated that he had constructed his human racial classification simply as a matter of convenience (*The Myth of Race,* 2014). I want you to hear that. Blumenbach's thesis was not based on empirical data or scientific fact but rather just his opinion.

Blumenbach went on to specify five categories of people associated with the major regions of the world. His definitions were: Caucasian, Mongoloid, Ethiopian, American, and Malay. These categories became widely accepted by the educated community. Although there have been some evolutions of these categories throughout the years, there still remains a rather fierce belief and adherence to some of Blumenbach's definitions, derived from his original thesis. Keep in mind, however, that his thesis was not based on any empirical data or scientific fact, but simply the opinion of one man.

I find it a fascinating phenomenon in the world that everything begins with thoughts in the individual minds of men. These thoughts, when articulated well and received by others, become the dogma by which society functions. Thoughts can be right or wrong; thoughts can be good or evil. They can be used to advance the cause of mankind in a righteous way or as poison to tear down the righteous advancement of mankind. I would say that the work of Mr. Blumenbach is one of those works that has served to create massive, systematic divisions, fragmentation, war, and oppression of entire people groups based on aesthetics—that is, the color of one's skin.

Blumenbach first coined the term "Caucasian" to refer to people of European descent and, in doing so, defined them as the most beautiful, the closest to representing God's image, and the original humans from which other varieties had degenerated. WOW! It is very important to note once again that this was done by no scientific means. He developed this on purely aesthetic-biased beliefs—his own views of aesthetics. Blumenbach's descriptions are biased by his own imprimatur of beauty. However, he presents his thesis as though he were discussing an objective and quantifiable property, not subject to doubt or disagreement (*Gould 1996, p. 411*). Think about this: Much of mankind's prejudicial beliefs, which are still alive and well today, had their origins in the minds of men centuries ago.

Around the same time, similar schools of thought

began to take root. Immanuel Kant, an 18th-century philosopher, also introduced into the academic world his intellectual and personally biased pursuit of defining men according to their skin color. Kant's theory of "Race" spoke to the intellectual abilities and limitations of the so-called races. Kant separated so-called races by a color code. Those being of Europe, Asia, Africa, and Native America were differentiated by their degree of innate talent in Kant's theory. The nature of the "White" race guarantees its rational and moral order as the highest position of all creatures, followed by "Yellow," "Black," and then "Red." According to Kant, "Nonwhites" do not have the capacity to realize reason and rational moral perfectibility through education. Therefore, skin color serves as evidence of unchanging and unchangeable moral quality and, thus, ultimately, of free will. Think about that! You may think, "This is the most absurd piece of BS I have ever read." But I guarantee you the tentacles of this belief system are still well intact and still serve to govern the thought processes of billions of people.

This is a thesis with massive implications for those whose so-called race was placed in a category of superiority. This would serve as an impetus to protect this line of thinking so that their so-called race could maintain a world-dominating posture in every sphere of activity, including religion, politics, economics, and social strata. For those who were placed in the lower categories of mankind, it would proliferate a belief system that they are "less than" and could never hope to achieve better. According to Kant, it is impossible, even through education, to improve the capacity of those of the nonwhite race to achieve intelligence and higher moral character than those of "Whites."

This is astonishing, and I hope it is eye-opening to all who are reading this text. Although this book is not written specifically for people of color, it is intended to bring enlightenment to all people. At this point, I must interject a vital line of thought.

Chapter 3: Mentalities

I believe that what I am about to say, though it may be more pronounced in African American life, is true in other cultures across the world. In the African American community, I grew up with the popular notion among melanated people: the concept of "Good and Bad" hair. If you had soft, straight, or curly hair, you had "Good hair." If your hair was thicker and coarse (what we called "Nappy)," you had "Bad hair." You see, this comes from cultural conditioning—and what a conditioning it has been and continues to be.

Ever since melanated people were brought to the shores of the Americas, we have been taught that "White is good," and the features of non-melanated people are good and to be desired. Does this sound familiar? See Chapter 2. This means that non-melanated features, such as facial features, skin tone, body shapes, and eye color, are considered desirable, and if you are not that, you are not good or desirable. I'm telling you—THIS IS TRUE in the psyche of melanated people. This is why many melanated women wear wigs that look like the hair of white or non-melanated folks. Wow! What an unpopular thing to say. Sadly, though, it is true.

The centuries-old, baked-in doctrine that "White is good" and "Black is bad" has had a generationally devastating effect on people of color around the world. The fact is that this doctrine, born out of Western culture, has permeated many cultures beyond the West. Girls in Asian cultures have now taken to bleaching their skin. There are all kinds of creams and bleaches they are employing, all in an effort to lighten their skin so they fit the "desirable model." These things are a direct result of the effects of the invention of RACE.

In the 1970s, an American entertainer used his celebrity and music to inject social commentary into the culture. One such song of social commentary was entitled, "Say it Loud, I'm Black and I'm Proud." His name was James Brown. This was such a needed infusion of self-worth for "Blacks" at the time. It provided a poignant counterpoint to the popular notion that "White is good and right" and "Black is bad and wrong." Again, this was the product of years of racist indoctrination into the minds of the masses. I find it somewhat humorous and puzzling that while people denounce certain others because of the dark color of their skin, some of these same people crave a good "sun tan."

I, for one, am glad to see many young people wearing their hair as God intended for them—not straightened or processed, not shaped to look like Europeans when they are not. Rather, many young men, in particular, are choosing to wear their hair naturally. To this, I say bravo. I hope that many women of color will begin to do the same and rejoice in whom God created them to be.

And there is more.

As I write this chapter today, it happens to be Juneteenth 2023. Parts of America are commemorating June 19th as the day millions of people with melanated skin were informed that they had been emancipated from slavery—two years prior to their receiving this knowledge! This, indeed, is part of the African American story, which is a unique story amongst all melanated people throughout the world. Although African American people were emancipated from slavery due to the edict of President Abraham Lincoln, it was not an emancipation filled with goodness, kindness, and benevolence from half of the people of America. The emancipation of slaves was met with disdain, anger, hatred, violence, and vehement resistance from many of the non-melanated persuasion.

No sooner had the Emancipation Proclamation been put into effect than another law was added to the Constitution of the United States: it is called the 13th Amendment. The 13th Amendment states that it is unlawful to enslave anyone in America or to force them to labor without pay, except if they are found guilty of a crime. Due to the fact that overnight, a workforce of four million people was removed from the working slave class of society (free labor), those in power had to come up with a way to get that workforce back or face the sure collapse of their economy. Without this mighty workforce, it would have meant economic ruin for many in the South and some in the North. Hence, the 13th Amendment would serve as a legal means to convict people of crimes, forcing them to labor, and not have to pay them.

People of color began to be arrested on trumped-up charges and forced to labor because they did not have the money to pay the fines that were imposed on them by the courts. So, you might imagine that it would be beneficial to arrest people for things like loitering. Black men were arrested by the dozens and assigned to work on the very plantations from which they were recently freed.

I would argue that this was the beginning of systematic imprisonment for the benefit of financial gain. The spirit of this injustice is still at work today in the country of my origin, which is America. All one would need to do is a cursory study of the statistics concerning the disproportionate amount of people of "color" who are incarcerated versus those of "non-color." Some would argue that systematic racism does not exist. I do not subscribe to that line of thinking. Although systems of racial discrimination have diminished significantly over the last 100 years in America, there still exist the marks of systematic racism—some more pronounced than others—yet it is still very real. And while this is still very real, I do not subscribe to melanated people using this as a reason not to attempt to better ourselves. There is no reason for people of color over the last 50 years not to take advantage of the opportunities afforded African Americans that were not afforded to our forefathers.

Even though a system is built in a way that does not afford people of color in America some of the same opportunities as their non-melanated counterparts, there are still certain internal qualities of a man that are the true determinants as to whether that man succeeds or fails.

As I stated at the outset of my book, I am well aware of the racial hatred that exists in people and have been a victim of it at various times and circumstances during my lifetime.

There is a big "however." I believe, as stated by the author Shelby Steele, "Personal responsibility is the brick and mortar of power. The responsible person knows that the quality of his life is something that he will have to make inside the limits of his fate. Some of these limits he can push back; some he cannot. But in any case, the quality of his life will pretty much reflect the quality of his efforts." (*The Content Of Our Character*, p.33).

The fact of the matter is that melanated people in America are free, and Mr. Steele further says the exhilaration of new freedom is always followed by a shock of accountability. This is a truism, and I have seen this firsthand in what has become part of my life's work. And now, onto a perspective of Personal Responsibility vs. Racism.

While systemic racism has undeniably shaped the lives of melanated people, an equally crucial element in their journey toward empowerment lies in embracing personal responsibility. This concept, though controversial in some circles, underlines the ability of individuals to rise above the limitations imposed by external structures. It requires an honest examination of how much of one's success can be attributed to effort, strategy, and mindset. For African Americans and other people of color, this perspective does not negate the reality of racial discrimination; rather, it challenges individuals to redefine their sense of self-worth and agency despite societal barriers.

Taking responsibility for one's life begins with understanding identity. From a young age, children are influenced by the stories and beliefs that their families and communities pass down to them. For many African Americans, these narratives often oscillate between a recognition of past struggles and an acknowledgment of present opportunities. The tension between these two perspectives creates a powerful dynamic. On the one hand, there is an acute awareness of the historical injustices that have hindered progress; on the other, there is the realization that present-day opportunities, though unequal, are still more abundant than those available to previous generations.

In the words of Nelson Mandela, "Education is the most powerful weapon which you can use to change the world." Education—formal or otherwise—offers a pathway to empowerment. Yet, education must extend beyond academic knowledge to include emotional intelligence, self-discipline, and an understanding of one's cultural heritage. These elements are critical for fostering resilience and a sense of purpose in a world that may not always be welcoming.

One of the most insidious effects of racism is its ability to erode self-esteem. The cultural conditioning that associates whiteness with beauty, intelligence, and moral superiority has long cast a shadow over melanated communities. This psychological warfare manifests in subtle ways, from media representation to workplace microaggressions. To combat these forces, it is essential to challenge internalized stereotypes and embrace an unapologetic celebration of one's identity.

This reclamation of identity can take many forms. For some, it involves reconnecting with ancestral traditions and histories that were erased or diminished by colonial narratives. For others, it's about defining success on their own terms, whether through entrepreneurship, artistry, or advocacy. What remains constant is the need to reject the notion that societal validation is necessary for self-worth.

Consider the recent resurgence of movements like #BlackGirlMagic and #BlackExcellence. These campaigns underscore the importance of visibility and representation in shaping identity. They remind melanated individuals that their contributions and achievements are worth celebrating, irrespective of the dominant cultural narrative. By creating their own symbols of success, people of color can inspire future generations to dream bigger and aim higher.

While acknowledging the structural inequities created by racism, it is also imperative to reframe the narrative around it. Racism should not be the defining element of one's existence. Instead, it should serve as a backdrop against which stories of triumph and resilience are told. This reframing requires a shift in focus: from oppression to opportunity, from victimhood to victory.

Communities play a pivotal role in fostering this shift. Historically, African American communities have thrived when they embraced collective responsibility. During the Reconstruction era, for example, freedmen and freedwomen established schools, churches, and businesses despite facing relentless hostility. These institutions became sanctuaries of learning, faith, and economic empowerment. They offered not only tangible resources but also a sense of pride and belonging.

Today's communities can draw inspiration from these examples. By prioritizing mentorship, skill-building, and mutual support, they can create environments where individuals feel empowered to take charge of their destinies. Programs that pair successful professionals with youth from underprivileged backgrounds are particularly effective in breaking cycles of poverty and despair. These relationships provide not just guidance but also a living testament to what is possible through determination and effort.

While personal responsibility is critical, it must be balanced with a commitment to advocacy. Structural racism cannot be dismantled by individual effort alone. Collective action—in the form of voting, protesting, and lobbying—remains essential for addressing systemic inequities. Advocacy ensures that institutions are held accountable for their role in perpetuating discrimination. It complements the work of personal development by creating a more equitable playing field for all.

This dual approach—combining self-improvement with societal reform—is evident in the lives of many historical figures. Martin Luther King Jr., for instance, exemplified the power of combining personal discipline with public activism. His commitment to nonviolent resistance was not just a strategy for achieving civil rights but also a testament to the moral authority that comes from living a principled life.

The struggle against racism is not confined to the United States. Around the world, people of color face varying degrees of discrimination and exclusion. However, their stories also offer valuable lessons in resilience and creativity.

In Brazil, the largest population of African descendants outside Africa continues to grapple with racial inequality. Yet, Afro-Brazilian communities have preserved and celebrated their heritage through music, dance, and religion. Practices like Capoeira and Candomblé serve as both cultural expressions and acts of resistance against a legacy of slavery.

Similarly, in the United Kingdom, Black Britons have made significant strides in sectors ranging from literature to politics. Their achievements underscore the importance of representation and the need for policies that address systemic disparities.

Whether in South Africa's post-apartheid era or India's caste-based hierarchies, the fight for equality shares common themes. Across these contexts, education emerges as a powerful tool for breaking down barriers. Grassroots movements often succeed when they combine local knowledge with global solidarity, reminding us that the quest for justice transcends borders.

As we reflect on the intersection of personal responsibility and systemic change, one thing becomes clear: the future is shaped by the choices we make today. For melanated communities, this means embracing both their heritage and their potential. It means rejecting the false dichotomy between acknowledging racism and pursuing personal excellence. Both are possible, and both are necessary.

The path forward requires a collective commitment to rewriting the narrative. It calls for celebrating achievements without ignoring challenges, for holding systems accountable while fostering individual growth. Most importantly, it demands that we see ourselves not as passive recipients of history but as active authors of our destiny.

To quote Maya Angelou: "You may encounter many

defeats, but you must not be defeated." These words remind us that resilience is not just about surviving adversity but about transforming it into a stepping stone for greater heights. In this spirit, let us move forward with courage, compassion, and an unwavering belief in the power of truth and responsibility to change the world.

Chapter 4: BBN

In 2009, I was called to pioneer and pastor a church in Newark, New Jersey. I believe that an integral part of any church must be to meet the "felt needs" (a term coined by John M. Perkins in his book *Beyond Charity*) of the community in which they find themselves. Not being from an inner-city environment, I was unsure about how the inner city functions or what might be their greatest needs. So, I set out to discover what the greatest needs were in the city where I felt God had called me to serve.

I began to develop relationships with elected officials in City Hall, including councilmen, the mayor, the business administrator, and the like. When I had the opportunity to speak with these individuals one-on-one, I would ask, "What do you think are the greatest needs of the city?" Their answers were always consistent. The number one concern was public safety, and the second was jobs. As I reflected on these consistent answers, it occurred to me that these two issues—public safety and jobs—are not mutually exclusive. They work hand in hand. Part of the solution to improving public safety would be to create jobs because the more people who have gainful employment, the less crime there is likely to be.

I set out to use the business acumen I had gained over a 20-year career in corporate America and owning my business for 16 years. I needed to find a way to help people who otherwise would not receive a hand-up. These are the folks with barriers to employment, such as a felony prison record, a lack of education, being undereducated, or the fact that they have never held a job. Some had never known what it was like to work in a structured nine-to-five company setting.

Through various network channels and a good dose of persistence, I was able to land a contract with a large project management firm in the commercial construction space for day laborers. This success came after a solid year of knocking on doors and making phone calls in an effort to enter into a contractual agreement with a construction firm to hire day laborers.

In 2014, Bridge Builders Newark was born. The company started with myself and a couple of other individuals going out into the field, performing manual labor functions at construction sites. I found myself working side by side with the people I hired, hauling trash, sweeping up, and carrying construction debris to the dumpster. This proved to be one of the most valuable lessons I could teach people who had no prior work experience: to show rather than just tell. By working alongside them and doing the same labor they were doing, I demonstrated the value of hard work and teamwork.

This approach proved to be very inspirational to many people who came to work for Bridge Builders Newark. To see the owner working side by side with them, just as hard as they worked, without thinking himself better than anyone, created unspoken motivation. They were motivated to work hard and get an honest day's pay for an honest day's work.

Since those early days, we have hired hundreds of people with barriers to employment and paid them a living wage. We have seen many people's lives transformed for the better, allowing them to live a better quality of life because they were willing to put in the effort. By the way, Bridge Builders Newark is a for-profit LLC company. Many people mistake our business for a nonprofit company because we exhibit such nonprofit values. However, we are indeed a for-profit limited liability corporation that, over the years, has hired hundreds of people and paid millions of dollars in salaries to people who otherwise more than likely would not have had that chance.

Now, getting back to the postulate of Shelby Steele, the actualization of new freedom is always followed by a shock of accountability. What I have witnessed is that, for people who have been incarcerated for an extended period— let's say, 5, 10, or 15 years. When they come out of prison, there may be an exhilaration that I am now free. However, almost immediately following that comes the shock of accountability. Now, no one is telling me when to wake up, when to go to work, when to go to the bathroom, when to eat, and so on and so on and so on.

A new reality hits: that now my functioning, and the order of my day-to-day life depend on me. And some people are just not ready for that.

We have hired people who are out of prison in less than two weeks. They appear to be healthy, focused, and willing to work. So many of them begin with a bang, and they do well. I have seen people get their own cars, get their own apartments, and things they never had prior to coming to work for Bridge Builders. But, there's a phenomenon that occurs that is saddening.

After a time, they begin to decrease in their performance. They begin to take days off, come late to work, or not at all, and without even a phone call. Basic things that the average working person would know are taboo. At Bridge Builders, all of these things are forgivable. We try to coach and teach our staff. We take the time to explain that there are certain disciplines necessary to maintain a job. Some of them learn these lessons, but the majority, sadly, do not. The majority feel that someone owes them something, and the majority feel that they can do the least amount of work, hoping to get the most amount of pay. This is a deeply ingrained mentality that affects many melanated people in the inner cities of America.

I know that it is incumbent upon me and my staff to communicate that no one owes you anything, and the only way that you are going to make a good life for yourself is to become self-sufficient and disciplined. To change such a mentality, one must put in the requisite effort to realize the benefits that would make for a better quality of life. It may seem odd to some who are reading this book that you would have to explain this to people. However, there is a lingering mentality amongst people from the African diaspora whose ancestors went through the transatlantic slave trade and, for generations, were beaten down and made to think that they are less than and incapable of achievement.

I would like to borrow another thesis put forth by Shelby Steele, and that is that due to this systematic degradation of melanated people, something called "the anti-self" is born, which is the unseen agent of low self-esteem.

This is the agent that robs people of color of their

Agency. I have always heard the saying that some people have a fear of failure, but what is just as true is that some people have a fear of success because with success comes responsibility. Therefore, I have seen people who begin to do well self-sabotage and revert back to the very thing, the very lifestyle, the very mindsets that put them in prison or in a poor quality of life because they are afraid of success.

Behind this fear of success lies the anti-self, the lack of belief that one can achieve whatever one sets their mind to. And a belief system that says "they" (the ominous they) will keep me down, will not let me succeed, will not let me achieve. So, they become the excuse for non-achievement.

When in reality the reason for non-achievement is because one has not been built up in who they were created to be, but I will talk more on this in the chapters to follow. All of this, both systemic racism and the anti-self, are rooted in the myth of Race!

The myth of race is one of the world's most powerful tools to enslave men, not only physically, but more insidious, is the mental toll it has taken on whole people groups.

However, there is an answer. And the answer is spiritual. Hold on to your hat.

The harmful mindsets rooted in racial conditioning have long perpetuated cycles of internalized racism, creating a pervasive undercurrent of self-doubt and inferiority within communities of color. These mindsets are not accidental; they are the result of centuries of systemic oppression and deliberate strategies designed to undermine the self-worth of entire populations. By examining these patterns and their origins, we can better understand the cultural and psychological hurdles that have arisen and explore the pathways toward healing and empowerment.

One of the most insidious aspects of racial conditioning is the establishment of beauty standards that favor whiteness. For example, the dichotomy of "good hair" versus "bad hair" reflects a broader global obsession with Eurocentric features. This preference is evident in Western societies and across the globe, where skin bleaching remains a multimillion-dollar industry in regions like Africa, Asia, and the Caribbean. These practices reveal a deep-seated belief that lighter skin equates to higher value, success, and desirability.

This phenomenon—the internalization of whiteness as the ideal—can be traced back to colonialism and the global spread of European cultural dominance. Colonizers imposed their values and aesthetics on the societies they subjugated, creating hierarchies that favored those who conformed to their standards. Over time, these imposed values became internalized, leading individuals to equate their natural features with inferiority. The result is a pervasive psychological struggle where people of color feel pressured to alter their appearance to fit a mold that was never designed to include them.

Cultural movements to reclaim identity and pride have emerged as powerful antidotes to this conditioning. For instance, James Brown's anthem, "Say It Loud, I'm Black and I'm Proud," became a rallying cry for self-acceptance during the Civil Rights Movement. This song and similar cultural expressions challenged the narrative of inferiority by celebrating Blackness in all its forms. Movements like these encouraged people to reject societal standards that devalued their identities and instead proudly embrace their heritage.

Despite such efforts, the remnants of internalized racism remain deeply embedded. This internalization manifests in subtle yet destructive ways, often as self-sabotage or the fear of success. As Shelby Steele's concept of the anti-self illustrates, these fears are not irrational but deeply rooted in historical and systemic oppression. The anti-self convinces individuals that they cannot achieve their goals or that external forces will thwart their efforts. This belief becomes a self-fulfilling prophecy, trapping people in cycles of stagnation and despair.

The cultural phenomenon of "crab mentality"—a metaphor derived from crabs in a bucket pulling each other down—is another symptom of internalized racism. When individuals within marginalized communities begin to rise above their circumstances, they are often met with resistance from their peers. This dynamic stems from a scarcity mindset, where people believe that success is finite and that another's gain diminishes their own potential. This destructive mentality perpetuates division and prevents collective progress.

The global obsession with whiteness is not limited to beauty standards; it extends to economic and social structures as well. In many societies, lighter-skinned individuals are more likely to receive better job opportunities, higher salaries, and social privileges. This colorism, a byproduct of racial conditioning, reinforces the notion that lighter skin is synonymous with competence and value. The message is clear for those who do not fit this mold: they are inherently less deserving.

This messaging begins early, often in childhood, and is reinforced through media, education, and interpersonal interactions. Consider the classic "doll test" psychologists Kenneth and Mamie Clark conducted in the 1940s. When presented with dolls of different skin tones, African American children overwhelmingly preferred the white dolls, associating them with positive traits like beauty and intelligence. This experiment, repeated with similar results decades later, highlights the enduring impact of racial conditioning on self-perception.

Addressing these challenges requires a multifaceted approach that combines cultural, psychological, and spiritual interventions. Cultural movements are critical in reshaping narratives and providing counterexamples to the dominant ideals. For example, the natural hair movement has empowered individuals to embrace their natural textures, challenging the notion that straight hair is superior. By normalizing diverse representations of beauty, such movements help dismantle the harmful stereotypes perpetuated by mainstream media.

Psychological interventions must address the internalized beliefs that underpin feelings of inferiority. This begins with education and awareness—helping individuals recognize the origins of these beliefs and their impact on behavior. Community-based initiatives that foster open dialogue and peer support can also be effective in creating environments where people feel safe to explore and challenge their internalized biases.

The journey toward self-worth is deeply personal yet profoundly collective. It requires individuals to confront their own anti-self and the fears that come with accountability and success. This confrontation is not easy; it demands vulnerability and resilience. However, the rewards—self-acceptance, empowerment, and the ability to break free from cycles of self-doubt—are immeasurable.

Spirituality offers another avenue for healing and transformation. For many, faith provides a framework for understanding their worth beyond societal standards. It reminds them that their value is inherent and not contingent on external validation. Spiritual practices such as meditation, prayer, and communal worship can be powerful tools for cultivating inner strength and resilience.

Healing also requires a reckoning with history. The scars of systemic racism cannot be erased, but they can be acknowledged and addressed. This process involves creating spaces where the stories of oppression and resilience can be shared and honored. By understanding the historical context of their struggles, individuals and communities can begin to dismantle the myths and narratives that have held them back.

Empowerment must also extend to structural changes. While individual transformation is critical, it must be accompanied by systemic reforms that address the root causes of inequality. This includes advocating for policies that promote equity in education, employment, and housing and challenging discriminatory practices in all their forms. By addressing both the personal and the structural dimensions of internalized racism, we can create a society where everyone has the opportunity to thrive.

The work of overcoming internalized racism is ongoing and multifaceted. It requires persistence, community support, and a willingness to confront uncomfortable truths. Yet, through this work, individuals can reclaim their identities, reject societal conditioning, and embrace their true selves. The journey is not without challenges, but the destination—a world where everyone is valued and empowered to reach their full potential—is well worth the effort.

Ultimately, the path to self-worth begins with rejecting the myth of race and embracing the reality of shared humanity. It requires us to look beyond the divisions imposed upon us and see ourselves and others as inherently valuable. By doing so, we can break free from the cycles of self-doubt and inferiority that have long plagued communities of color and create a future rooted in equity, dignity, and mutual respect.

Chapter 5: Division Is Our Problem

Although we spent some time in the last chapter unpacking the facts that have plagued people of the African American experience—and, more broadly, the African American diaspora—I want to shift gears here to explore the problem of "race," which blankets our world like a plague. While several significant factors contribute to the division, separation, prejudice, and hatred among the world's people groups, I want to address one of the most diabolical: skin color.

One of the greatest tragedies of this diabolical division is its ability to manipulate not just how we view others but also how we view ourselves. Skin color, a biological trait that should signify nothing more than the beautiful diversity of human creation, has become a weapon of systemic dehumanization. In America, this weapon was forged during the era of slavery and refined through the subsequent centuries of segregation, discrimination, and marginalization. Yet, as I write this, I recognize that the roots of this mindset run far more profound than the soil of America alone. Across the globe, differences in appearance—whether in complexion, hair texture, or facial features—have been exploited to create hierarchies of worth.

This exploitation often stems from a fundamental misunderstanding—or deliberate ignorance—of humanity's shared origins. If we return to the beginning, we see the truth of who we are. Genesis offers us a profound lens through which to understand our collective identity. Adam and Eve, created in the image and likeness of God, were the progenitors of all mankind. This divine truth reveals a critical fact: humanity was born unified, not divided. It was only through the fall—through sin and the subsequent corruption of human nature—that division emerged. The notion of "race," as it is wielded today, is a byproduct of this corruption, a tool used by man to elevate some while subjugating others.

From an American perspective, "color prejudice" has been a central theme since the first African slaves were brought to the colonies in 1619. This historical moment marked the beginning of a brutal narrative that sought to strip African people of their identity, reduce them to commodities, and justify their treatment through pseudoscientific theories of racial superiority. However, America is not alone in its struggle with prejudice. Across the world, tribalism, nationalism, and religious zealotry have similarly bred hatred and violence. The Rwandan genocide, the caste system in India, and the persecution of religious minorities are all stark reminders that division takes many forms, and not all of them center on color.

Yet, even as we condemn these atrocities, we must acknowledge an uncomfortable truth: division is seductive. It offers a false sense of superiority and belonging to those who cling to it. But this belonging is counterfeit, built on the exclusion and degradation of others. The Torah reminds us that God does not endorse such division. When humanity united to build the Tower of Babel, it was not their unity but their collective defiance of God's will that prompted Him to scatter them and confuse their languages. His actions were not punitive but corrective, a reminder that unity without righteousness is no unity.

In America and the wider world, we face a similar choice today. Will we allow the false unity of division—based on color, culture, or creed—to dictate our interactions? Or will we embrace the unity that comes from recognizing our shared humanity? The answer lies not in ignoring our differences but in celebrating them as reflections of the Creator's infinite imagination.

This requires us to reject the simplistic and reductive labels imposed upon us. Terms like "black," "white," "yellow," and "red" do little to capture the richness of individual identity. Worse, they perpetuate the myth that these superficial differences matter more than the truth that binds us. That truth, as the Scriptures affirm, is that we are all fearfully and wonderfully made in the image of God.

By embracing this truth, we can dismantle the systems and mindsets perpetuating division. This work is not easy. It demands introspection, humility, and a willingness to confront the lies we have been told—and the lies we have told ourselves. But moving closer to the world God intended is necessary, where division is replaced by understanding and hatred by love.

In North America, color prejudice began with massive discrimination and atrocities against the indigenous people who occupied the land. To the credit of the US, some attempts have been made to care for the Native People and repair damages through reparations and the like. However, the aftermath of systematic racism is still felt by those we refer to as Native Americans.

The concept of "color prejudice" began in 1619 with the American experiment on racial hierarchy. However, in other parts of the world, color is not the premier source of bigotry and hatred. It may be tribal, nationalistic, religious, or socio-economic. There have been and continue to be atrocities perpetuated: mankind against mankind, and the aforementioned have nothing to do with color. These would be white-on-white, black-on-black, red-on-red, yellow-on-yellow. It strikes me that the mere fact that I'm using these terms to describe people groups is a farce. But these terms I grew up with have been ingrained in my mind and yours.

Here is where I hope not to lose you. Whether you are African, Asian, European, Indian, Jewish, Christian, Muslim, Buddhist, Atheist, or something else, allow me to refer to a holy book that offers an answer to the evil alchemy of race and racism.

I thank God for the opportunity to share His truth (The Truth) with you because His word is truth. The Torah and Tanach—the laws and the prophets—are professed as *the* truth. Let's jump right into it because I want to talk to you about origins and true identity today.

Many labels and categorizations in the world seek to define people and tell us who we are. But we never truly know who we are until the word of God reveals it to us. We must discover God's view of man, not man's view of man.

The Scriptures say that when God created man—Adam and Eve—He called them "good." Everything that God created was good. This goodness had nothing to do with color, economic, political, or social status. These systems of measurement were not even in place. Yet God said to His creation, male and female, "You are already good because you are created in My image and likeness."

God's view of man is that man was created good, and I want to emphasize that man was created good, but with time, there was a fall. There was a falling away from God, and from that falling away from God by his original man, Adam and Eve, many things transpired. Many things changed, and no sooner did that fall occur than there was a dividing line between men and women. You can read Genesis chapter 3. There, you will discover the birth of "At that moment, the nature of man shifted from good to bad. Our nature has since existed in a state of utter corruption.

Today, we see divisions in language, ethnicity, nationality, culture, politics, gender, and more. All these factors contribute to division among people. Let's explore one fascinating example: language.

The Torah teaches that Hashem (God) confused the languages of men. After Noah and his family survived the flood and emerged from the ark, they were the only surviving people on the planet. God had judged mankind because "the heart of man was only wickedness continually."

They all spoke the same language. If we pick up human history after the flood where they all would have spoken the same language. Their descendants would have spoken the same language. Until one day, they had this big idea that they were going to ascend to the throne of heaven, and they were going to take over heaven. They're going to become gods.

A result of a fallen, corrupt mindset. In response, God said, "No, you're not." He thwarted their plan with ease by confusing their languages. Suddenly, people could no longer understand each other. This created distinct people groups, divided along family lines. Noah had three sons: Shem, Ham, and Japheth. The consequences of this massive intervention by God in human affairs will be explored further in this book. For now, suffice it to say that language became the first separating factor for three people groups: the descendants of Shem, Ham, and Japheth.

The Torah explains that God dispersed these groups to different parts of the earth. While God instituted the language barrier, it is essential to understand that Yah does not desire division. However, when men unite in agreement for evil, God ensures their plans only go so far.

And, although throughout the millennia, gross atrocities have been perpetrated by humanity upon one another, all empires come to an end, and Yahuwah will eventually judge and cleanse the earth of all evil. For your further reference, this may be verified by reading the Prophet Isaiah in the Tanach.

The division initiated by the confusion of languages at Babel may have started as a means of thwarting human arrogance. Still, these separations hardened over time into cultural and societal boundaries that mankind weaponized for dominance. The descendants of Shem, Ham, and Japheth, each assigned to their respective regions, developed distinct customs, languages, and ways of life. Initially, this diversity could have been a reflection of God's creativity and the adaptability of humans to different environments. Yet, as time passed, the differences that should have been celebrated became the basis for hierarchies, exclusion, and systemic oppression.

One of the most striking examples is the development of racial theories in the 18th and 19th centuries. Figures like Johann Friedrich Blumenbach, with his arbitrary classification of humans into five races, and Immanuel Kant, with his disturbing assertions about the moral and intellectual capacities of non-white groups, gave a veneer of scientific legitimacy to prejudices that already existed. These ideas, built not on empirical evidence but on personal biases, influenced policies and institutions that entrenched inequality. From the transatlantic slave trade to colonialism, the fabricated concept of racial superiority justified some of history's greatest atrocities.

These pseudo-scientific theories were not merely abstract ideas confined to academia. They seeped into the cultural consciousness, shaping how entire societies viewed themselves and others. For people of African descent, these ideologies became shackles not only of the body but of the mind. The systemic dehumanization, which began with physical enslavement, extended into psychological captivity that reinforced feelings of inferiority. For the oppressors, these ideas offered justification for greed and exploitation, perpetuating cycles of violence and oppression that spanned generations.

But as much as the myth of race has been used to divide us, it also serves as a reminder of our shared humanity. If we return to the story of Noah, we see that all humanity shares a common lineage. Every culture, language, and phenotype ultimately traces back to the same source. This is not just a theological or philosophical assertion but a scientific fact. Genetic studies confirm that the differences in our appearances are superficial, accounting for only a minuscule fraction of our genetic makeup. Beneath our skin, we are far more alike than we are different.

Recognizing this truth should compel us to dismantle the barriers we have created. However, this process requires more than an intellectual acknowledgment of our shared humanity. It demands a transformation of the heart. The divisions that plague us are rooted not just in ignorance but in pride, fear, and the fallen nature of man. Overcoming these requires more than human effort; it requires divine intervention.

The Scriptures repeatedly call us to unity. Paul's letter to the Galatians reminds us that in Christ, "there is neither Jew nor Greek, slave nor free, male nor female, for you are all one in Christ Jesus." This radical equality challenges the societal structures that seek to divide us. It is a call to see one another not through the lens of race, class, or nationality but as brothers and sisters, equally valued and loved by God.

Yet, achieving this vision of unity is no small task. It requires us to confront the uncomfortable truths of our history and how we continue to perpetuate division. In America, for example, the legacy of slavery and segregation still casts a long shadow. The current economic, social, and political inequalities are not accidents of history but the deliberate result of policies and practices designed to exclude and marginalize. Acknowledging this is not about assigning blame but understanding the roots of our present challenges so we can address them effectively.

It also requires us to examine our own hearts. Division is not just a systemic issue; it is a personal one. We carry biases and prejudices, often unconsciously, that influence how we see and treat others. Overcoming these requires humility—a willingness to listen, learn, and change. It requires us to be honest about how we have contributed to division, whether through our actions, words, or silence.

Faith communities have a unique role to play in this work. At their best, they can be spaces where people of different backgrounds come together to worship, serve, and grow. They can model the kind of unity the world so desperately needs, showing that bridging divides and building relationships based on mutual respect and love is possible. But for this to happen, they must also be willing to confront their own shortcomings. Too often, faith communities have mirrored the divisions of the broader society rather than challenging them. The words of Dr. Martin Luther King Jr. still ring true: "It is appalling that the most segregated hour of Christian America is eleven o'clock on Sunday morning."

The work of healing division is long and arduous, but it is also profoundly hopeful. History is filled with examples of individuals and movements that defied the odds to unite people. The abolitionist movement, the Civil Rights Movement, and the Truth and Reconciliation Commission in South Africa are just a few examples of what is possible when people commit themselves to justice and reconciliation. These efforts remind us that change is possible, even amid entrenched systems and seemingly insurmountable odds.

As we look to the future, we must hold onto this hope. We must believe that a more just and united world is possible and inevitable, for it is the world God has promised. In the words of the prophet Micah, "He has shown you, O mortal, what is good. And what does the Lord require of you? To act justly, love mercy, and walk humbly with your God."

This is our calling. To act justly, we must confront the division and inequality systems surrounding us. To love mercy, we must extend grace to those who have wronged us and seek reconciliation where there has been hurt. And to walk humbly with our God, we must recognize that we cannot do this work alone. It is only through His strength, His wisdom, and His love that we can hope to overcome the divisions that plague our world.

Let us commit ourselves to this work, knowing it is not in vain. For in every act of justice, every gesture of mercy, and every step of humility, we bring the kingdom of God a little closer. And in doing so, we reclaim our shared humanity and reflect the unity God always intended for His creation.

Chapter 6: "Race"

Let's continue examining the various kinds of dividing lines among mankind. We have socioeconomic division, religious division, and tribal division; all of these mechanisms are designed to keep people separate and at odds with one another. Mankind is thoroughly divided at this point. We can observe the world around us and easily identify examples of these divisions. The current global narrative clearly demonstrates that the issues dividing us are on an ever-increasing upward trajectory.

We seem to find ways to be vehemently divided over seemingly anything. It has taken me years to complete this book. However, as I write this chapter, the world is in the throes of the COVID-19 pandemic. People are divided today over matters as basic as whether or not to wear a mask. Some individuals become angry when someone chooses to wear a mask, while others take offense when someone chooses not to. I understand there is a larger backdrop to this debate, involving the pandemic and its far-reaching implications. Still, this is yet another example of how issues are weaponized to divide us.

I'm not going to get political here because the issue of masks has evolved into a political matter rather than a purely health-related one. I use this merely as an illustration of how countless things are set up to pit people against one another. By the way, when I say "men," I mean mankind—both men and women, of course. ☺

While these divisions are pervasive, the most

significant dividing line throughout history has been "color." The color of one's skin remains the most potent source of division among mankind. To illustrate this, consider a quote attributed to former U.S. President Lyndon B. Johnson:

"If you can convince the lowest white man he's better than the best-colored man, he won't notice you're picking his pocket. Give him somebody to look down on, and he'll empty his pockets for you."

Notice the emphasis on color in Johnson's statement. The suggestion is that if you can convince the lowest white man that he is inherently superior to the best-colored man, he will overlook being manipulated and exploited. There's a sinister strategy at work here—a plot to gain political and financial power over the masses by using race as a divisive tool. This tactic encourages one group to look down on another, fueling a cycle of division and oppression.

A significant portion of the global population has adopted and perpetuated this ideology, finding ways to support, justify, and sustain it. When we reflect on President Johnson's quote and the issue of race, we see an underlying irony: he speaks of convincing a "white man" of his superiority, yet white itself is merely a color.

Those who are lost—operating under a fallen system—cling to this distorted perspective. They think of white as one thing and everyone else as another. However, this is a flawed and fallen mindset, rooted in the "fallen nature of the world" we discussed earlier.

Systemic racism in America has deep roots, extending back to the founding of the nation. While the abolition of slavery in 1865 with the 13th Amendment marked a significant milestone, it did not erase the systemic structures that perpetuated inequality. Instead, new mechanisms of oppression were instituted, maintaining the racial hierarchy and ensuring that African Americans and other marginalized groups remained subordinate in society. By examining the evolution of systemic racism from the post-slavery era to the present, we can better understand its persistent impact and explore how individuals and organizations can contribute to meaningful change.

The 13th Amendment formally abolished slavery, but it contained a critical loophole: "except as a punishment for crime." This clause laid the groundwork for a system of convict leasing, wherein African Americans, disproportionately arrested and convicted for minor offenses, were effectively re-enslaved. Southern states exploited this system, using the incarcerated to rebuild economies devastated by the Civil War. African Americans were arrested en masse for fabricated charges, such as vagrancy or loitering, and subjected to brutal working conditions. Following the Reconstruction era, the rise of Jim Crow laws further cemented racial inequality. These laws enforced segregation in schools, public transportation, housing, and virtually every aspect of public life. African Americans were denied access to quality education, healthcare, and employment opportunities, relegating them to a second-class status. The Supreme Court's infamous 1896 decision in Plessy v. Ferguson, which upheld the "separate but equal" doctrine, provided legal justification for segregation and legitimized systemic racism for decades.

Although the Civil Rights Movement dismantled many overt forms of racial discrimination, systemic racism persists in more insidious forms. Today, issues like mass incarceration, economic disparities, and employment barriers highlight the enduring effects of these entrenched systems. The United States has the highest incarceration rate in the world, and people of color are disproportionately represented in the prison population. African Americans make up roughly 13% of the U.S. population but account for nearly 40% of those incarcerated. The War on Drugs, initiated in the 1980s, played a significant role in this disparity. Policies such as mandatory minimum sentences and three-strikes laws disproportionately affected African American communities, where drug-related offenses were more heavily policed. The school-to-prison pipeline further exacerbates this issue. African American students are more likely to face suspension, expulsion, and referral to law enforcement for behavioral issues compared to their white peers. These punitive measures increase the likelihood of involvement in the criminal justice system, perpetuating cycles of poverty and disenfranchisement.

Economic inequality remains a defining feature of systemic racism. African Americans face significant barriers to accumulating wealth, stemming from historical practices like redlining and discriminatory lending. In the mid-20th century, the Federal Housing Administration systematically denied mortgages to African Americans, effectively excluding them from the post-war housing boom that created wealth for millions of white Americans. Today, the racial wealth gap persists, with the median white household holding nearly 10 times the wealth of the median Black household. This disparity is exacerbated by unequal access to education, lower wages for comparable work, and limited opportunities for upward mobility. Economic inequality not only affects individuals but also perpetuates disparities across generations, as wealth is a key determinant of access to quality education, healthcare, and other resources.

Employment discrimination continues to hinder economic progress for African Americans. Studies have consistently shown that job applicants with "white-sounding" names are more likely to receive callbacks for interviews than those with "Black-sounding" names, even when qualifications are identical. Furthermore, African Americans are often concentrated in low-wage, precarious jobs with limited opportunities for advancement. Structural barriers also play a role. African Americans are less likely to have access to professional networks, mentorship opportunities, and resources that facilitate career growth. This exclusion perpetuates a cycle of underrepresentation in higher-paying fields and leadership positions.

Addressing systemic racism requires both systemic reforms and grassroots initiatives. My work with Bridge Builders Newark highlights how community-based efforts can create opportunities and empower individuals to overcome systemic barriers. Newark, New Jersey, is a city with a rich history but also significant challenges, including high unemployment rates and economic disparities. Many residents face systemic barriers to employment, from a lack of access to quality education and job training to discrimination in hiring practices. Bridge Builders Newark was founded to address these challenges and create pathways to success for individuals in the community. One of our key initiatives is a workforce development program that provides job training, mentorship, and placement services for residents of Newark. Recognizing that many participants have been excluded from traditional employment opportunities due to systemic racism, we focus on building skills and fostering connections that help individuals secure stable, well-paying jobs. For example, we partner with local businesses to create apprenticeship programs, providing hands-on experience and a direct pipeline to employment.

Another important aspect of our work is addressing the unique challenges faced by formerly incarcerated individuals. As previously mentioned, mass incarceration disproportionately affects African Americans, and a criminal record can be a significant barrier to employment. Through our reentry program, we provide job training, resume-building workshops, and connections to employers willing to give second chances. By helping individuals reintegrate into the workforce, we aim to break the cycle of recidivism and create opportunities for economic stability. Our efforts also extend to addressing educational disparities. Bridge Builders Newark collaborates with local schools to provide mentorship programs for students, focusing on career readiness and financial literacy. By equipping young people with the skills and knowledge they need to succeed, we aim to disrupt the cycle of poverty and create pathways to upward mobility.

The examples above demonstrate that systemic racism continues to act as a barrier to progress, affecting every aspect of life for marginalized communities. However, they also highlight the potential for change through individual and collective action. While systemic issues require systemic solutions, individuals have the power to make a difference by creating opportunities, challenging discriminatory practices, and advocating for policy changes. Despite the overwhelming challenges posed by systemic racism, personal responsibility, and opportunity can offer paths forward. It is essential to acknowledge the resilience and agency of individuals who navigate these systems and work to create change in their own lives and communities. For example, participants in Bridge Builders Newark often demonstrate remarkable determination to overcome barriers to success. By taking advantage of available resources, building new skills, and seizing opportunities, they are able to achieve economic stability and inspire others in their communities. These individual successes, while not a solution to systemic issues, represent an important step toward broader change.

The persistence of systemic racism underscores the need for continued advocacy and reform. At the same time, individual action plays a crucial role in creating opportunities and driving change. Organizations like Bridge Builders Newark demonstrate that while the systems may be stacked against marginalized communities, personal responsibility, collective effort, and targeted interventions can help dismantle barriers and pave the way for progress. Addressing systemic racism requires a multifaceted approach that combines policy reforms, community-based initiatives, and individual empowerment. By working together, we can challenge the structures that perpetuate inequality and create a more equitable society for future generations.

The 13th Amendment's abolition of slavery, though a monumental achievement, introduced a critical loophole that was exploited to perpetuate racial inequalities. By allowing forced labor as punishment for a crime, this clause set the stage for practices like convict leasing. This exploitation disproportionately targeted African Americans, many of whom were arrested on fabricated or exaggerated charges, ensuring a supply of cheap labor. These practices served as an extension of slavery under another name, and they provided economic incentives to maintain discriminatory policies that systematically oppressed Black communities. These early examples of systemic racism laid the foundation for a society that continues to marginalize African Americans through institutionalized inequality.

Jim Crow laws that followed Reconstruction institutionalized segregation and discrimination, further entrenching the systemic barriers faced by African Americans. These laws relegated Black Americans to inferior facilities, schools, and opportunities, enforcing a narrative of racial inferiority. The Supreme Court's endorsement of these practices in Plessy v. Ferguson perpetuated a culture of separation and inequality. While these laws were eventually overturned, the ideology they promoted left a lasting imprint on American society, influencing policies and attitudes long after their formal repeal.

Today, the criminal justice system remains a potent instrument of systemic racism. The War on Drugs disproportionately targeted African Americans, with harsher sentences for offenses involving substances like crack cocaine, commonly associated with Black communities, compared to powdered cocaine, more prevalent in white communities. This disparity in sentencing contributed to the dramatic overrepresentation of African Americans in the prison population, disrupting families and eroding community stability. The consequences of mass incarceration extend beyond imprisonment, as individuals with criminal records face lifelong barriers to employment, housing, and civic participation. These systemic issues highlight the need for comprehensive reform to address the inequities perpetuated by the justice system.

Economic disparities are another manifestation of systemic racism, rooted in historical practices that excluded African Americans from wealth-building opportunities. Redlining, a practice that denied mortgages and loans to residents of predominantly Black neighborhoods, systematically prevented African Americans from accessing homeownership and the associated generational wealth. This exclusion created a wealth gap that persists today, with African Americans owning a fraction of the wealth held by their white counterparts. Discriminatory employment practices and wage gaps further compound these economic inequities, limiting the opportunities available to Black individuals and communities. Addressing these disparities requires dismantling the structural barriers that hinder economic mobility and implementing policies that promote equity and inclusion.

Education plays a pivotal role in perpetuating or addressing systemic racism. Historically, African Americans were denied access to quality education, a legacy that continues to affect educational outcomes today. Schools in predominantly Black neighborhoods often receive fewer resources, resulting in overcrowded classrooms, underpaid teachers, and outdated materials. These disparities contribute to achievement gaps that limit opportunities for higher education and career advancement. Initiatives that prioritize equitable funding, access to advanced coursework, and support for underrepresented students are essential to addressing these systemic issues and promoting educational equity.

Employment discrimination remains a significant barrier to economic progress for African Americans. Biases in hiring practices, often unconscious, disadvantage Black applicants, who are less likely to be called for interviews even when their qualifications are equivalent to those of white applicants. This discrimination extends to promotions and leadership opportunities, resulting in the underrepresentation of African Americans in higher-paying positions and industries. Programs that promote diversity, equity, and inclusion in the workplace are critical to addressing these disparities and creating environments where all individuals can thrive. Additionally, mentorship and networking opportunities can help bridge the gap, providing support and guidance for African Americans navigating systemic barriers in their careers.

Ultimately, addressing systemic racism requires a comprehensive approach that combines policy reforms, community initiatives, and individual empowerment. By challenging discriminatory practices, promoting equity, and supporting marginalized communities, we can create a more inclusive society. The work of organizations like Bridge Builders Newark demonstrates that progress is possible when individuals and communities come together to confront systemic barriers and build a future rooted in justice and equality. By continuing to advocate for change and support those affected by systemic racism, we can move closer to realizing the promise of equality for all.

Chapter 7: "The Answer"

If you have read this far, I trust you are tracking with me. So let me state unequivocally that there is an answer to this diabolical, demonically inspired thing called race. This answer is not found in the systems devised by mankind's ideologies or movements but in the transformative power of the Spirit of God. It is a truth that transcends the superficial divisions of skin color, ethnicity, and cultural heritage, and it calls us to a higher reality—one rooted in the divine nature of Christ Jesus, Yeshua.

As previously stated, there will be some who will hold to their deeply entrenched belief system of "Race and Racism." These systems, though pervasive and powerful, are not eternal. They are constructs of a fallen world, tools of division that have been wielded to oppress, dehumanize, and separate.

However, I trust that the God and Father of our Lord Jesus, the Anointed One, has given us a down payment on the earth (His Ruach/Breath/Holy Spirit). And those who partake of His Spirit will be shining examples of the Chosen, the Redeemed. Those who are not defined by the color of their skin, their socioeconomic status, or their cultural background.

These are the ones who are defined by their identity in Christ. This identity is not a mere label; it is a radical reorientation of one's entire being. It is a liberation from the false narratives of race and racism, a liberation that empowers us to live as salt and light in a world desperately in need of both. Those who have been changed by the power of His Spirit that has come to dwell within their hearts.

The limitations of human categorization do not confine this Spirit. It is a unifying force, a divine presence that transforms hearts and minds, enabling us to see beyond the artificial boundaries of race.

If this grace of God has hit your life and you are now able to live free of the ugly stain of race and racism, you have become the salt of the earth and the light of the world.

You have been set free to live as a reconciler, a peacemaker, and a bearer of divine truth. This freedom is not passive; it is active. It requires us to divest ourselves from the systems and ideologies that perpetuate division. It calls us to "come out from among them and be separate," not in a spirit of elitism or exclusion, but in a spirit of holiness and love.

Those of us who fit this bill can divest ourselves from the bondage of race and racism, no matter how large this curse looms over the earth. This is why the Lord would say, "Come out from among them and be separate." By the grace of God-Elohim, we are equipped to drop our guard. We are no longer defensive and angry. We do not immediately size people up and make pre-determined judgments about people based on the color of their skin. But, we are able to wait and access them on the content of their character.

We are now free to live life from a place that emanates from a pure and changed heart. Not from a place of false indoctrination or hurt from past experiences. This is the place of freedom. This is the place of true power, not living with anger, hostility, vengeance, and hatred for the things that were done to you and things that were done perhaps to your ancestors. We cannot live with this kind of emotional and spiritual baggage and expect to experience power.

I think that many movements across the world today are led from a place of anger, hatred, and hostility. This is not Christ or the Gospel. There is a better posture from which to express truth and justice. We must be able to express truth without a certain level of vitriol, which does not lead to persuasion or peace. We can and must speak truth and justice, but not emanating from the place of anger and hurt. We (The Righteousness of Yah/God) speak from a place of loving truth.

If you're reconciled to God, you are now called a reconciler. Think about it. If others are brought to the saving knowledge of the truth, then they would govern differently; people in political offices would govern and legislate according to righteousness.

Their political ideology would not be their hegemon. Leaders would legislate according to righteousness. Teachers in schools would teach according to righteousness. People in the neighborhood would treat each other according to righteousness. If people walked like this, they would do business differently. They wouldn't shut people out because they realized we're all one.

Don't think me Pollyannaish or cumbayish because I realize that on a global scale, this is not going to happen. There's not going to all of a sudden be a cumbaya moment, and everybody in the world sees this truth. This massive, global change will not transpire until the "End" comes.

When the end comes, God is going to do away with all of this darkness, ugliness, nastiness, deep-seated hatred, murder, enmity, and division between mankind. Yah is going to fix it all. Until then, we're called to spread righteousness because we have become the righteousness of God in Christ Jesus.

This is who we are. We are one in him. We are his righteousness. All are one in Christ. No matter what box people have tried to put you in, you're not in that box. If you're in Christ Jesus, you do not subscribe to the societal group think, or what they say. "They" (whoever they are) try (and quite successfully to put you in a "Black box," or "White box," an "Asian box," a "Hispanic box," a "Poor box," a "Rich box," a "Socio-economically challenged box," or an "Educational box." These are the things that are no longer your definers.

I pray by the spirit of God that you can hear what I'm about to say: This is true. While I exist in this skin of color, I am not a person of color. I am in Christ, and whatever color you may be, whether that's black color, brown color, white color, red color, or yellow color, you are no longer bound by this hegemon. Your color is not your guide. If God's Spirit, the Spirit of Christ Jesus, has come to live in you, He is your guide. It must be Him, His truth, His principles, His doctrine, precepts, and laws that are our hegemon.

When this becomes received and not only perceived truth in your soul, you will walk through life not as one whose self-imposed perception is second class, not buying into the narrative that you're second class but knowing who you are in Christ Jesus. When the realization that the God and Father of us all did not invent race (we did) and imbibe who we really are, then the notion of not labeling and defining myself as, ie. White will not be a quixotic notion.

If you embrace this, it will change your life. It will change your posture. It will change the way you walk. It will change the way you approach problems systemically, even in the workplace. I get it. There are a lot of things that are set up to keep one people group on top and keep other people group down. Yeah, it's all setup. But So what? In Christ Jesus, we have peace. In Christ Jesus, we can accomplish things, even if there are systems set up. Don't get me wrong.

To my reader, I am a man of "Color." I grew up in the United States and went to private school all my life, where I was a minority in a big way. This is the environment in which I was raised, so you can imagine I've experienced prejudice and racism of all kinds.

Oh yes, so I'm not a fool. I know what's out there. But I choose to put the Word of God on top. I choose to give the Word of Yah the preeminence in my life. I choose to live through the Word of God, not the way the world has framed me, not the way the media may portray me.

Whatever people group you may find yourself in, how your country looks at you is not the TRUE DEFINITION of YOU. True definition, your true definition comes from the Word of God. Let the word of God be front and center, and let him teach you who you are, how to live, and how to treat other people.

I'm talking to you whether you're rich, whether you are an elected politician, a banker, you're on Skid Row, or whether you're in the ghettos across the country. I'm talking to you because all are one in Christ Jesus, and this word (Hallelujah) applies to everyone across the globe. No exceptions for those who are the Righteousness of God.

A word of caution. I borrow again from the epic debate and postulate set forth by James Baldwin, whom we spoke of earlier. To the "Global Majority" who are actually and factually people of "Color" (mine), "The mind is incessantly trapped by the demoralizing treatment your country has systematically inflicted upon you purely because of the color of your skin: by the police, the taxi driver, the waiters, the landlord, the landlady, the banks, the insurance companies." And thousands of other microaggression experiences across decades of one life (mine) "That spell out to you that you are a worthless human being." Let not your heart be troubled, neither let it be afraid. You are created in the image of Him, who created all things. And you are equal in every way with every other people group on the planet.

To the "Global Minority" who are so-called "Whites" who have ruled for centuries, and not always by just means. "The proposition of equality does not pose a real proposition if one's system of reality does not make room for the notion" (Baldwin). My prayer for you is that, as a people, you will come out of the inveterate positions that have seemed to serve you well but polluted your soul.

I pray that you are blessed by hearing of His word via my small attempt to place His truth into the global narrative. It is my prayer that having now been exposed to the truth, we as mankind (some of us – prayerfully, many of us) will receive the truth. The Book says, "You will know the truth, and the truth will make you free." Free of all hate, racism, pre-judgment, bigotry, and racist vitriol, all built on the absolutely wicked alchemy and the false temple of "Race."

Let us walk in this truth, not as people defined by the divisions of this world but as people defined by the love and righteousness of Christ. Let us be reconcilers, peacemakers, and bearers of His light in a world that desperately needs it. And let us hold fast to the hope that one day, all things will be made new, and every division will be erased in the glory of His presence.

The struggle against race and racism is not merely a social or political battle; it is a spiritual one. At its core, it is a clash between the kingdom of darkness and the Kingdom of Light. The enemy has long used race as a weapon to divide humanity, sow discord, and perpetuate systems of oppression. But the Gospel of Jesus Christ is the ultimate antidote to this poison. It is a message of reconciliation, unity, and love that transcends all human divisions.

When we speak of race, we must recognize that it is a man-made construct, a flawed attempt to categorize and classify people based on superficial differences. But in the eyes of God, there is only one race—the human race. We are all descendants of Adam and Eve, all created in the image of God, and all equally in need of His grace. The divisions we see around us—whether racial, ethnic, or cultural—are not part of God's original design. They are the result of sin, brokenness, and the fall of humanity.

Yet, even in the midst of this brokenness, God has provided a way forward. Through the life, death, and resurrection of Jesus Christ, He has made it possible for us to be reconciled not only to Himself but also to one another. The cross is the great equalizer. It demolishes the walls of hostility that separate us and creates in its place a new humanity united in Christ.

As the apostle Paul declared, *"There is neither Jew nor Gentile, neither slave nor free, nor is there male and female, for you are all one in Christ Jesus"* (Galatians 3:28).

This unity is not something we can achieve on our own. It is a work of the Holy Spirit, who transforms our hearts and minds, enabling us to see one another through the eyes of Christ. When we are filled with His Spirit, we begin to love what He loves and value what He values. We no longer see people as "other" or "less than." Instead, we see them as brothers and sisters, fellow heirs of the grace of God.

This transformation has profound implications for how we live our lives. It challenges us to confront the prejudices and biases that we may have inherited or internalized. It calls us to actively resist the systems and structures that perpetuate inequality and injustice. And it compels us to be agents of reconciliation in a divided world. As followers of Christ, we are called to be peacemakers, to bridge the gaps that separate us, and to demonstrate the love of Christ in tangible ways.

But let us be clear: this does not mean ignoring or minimizing the very real pain and suffering that racism has caused. The wounds of racism run deep, and they cannot be healed with superficial solutions or empty platitudes. True reconciliation requires honesty, humility, and a willingness to listen and learn from those who have been marginalized and oppressed. It requires us to acknowledge the ways in which we have benefited from systems of privilege and to use our influence to advocate for justice and equality.

At the same time, we must guard against the temptation to respond to racism with hatred or bitterness. While anger is a natural and understandable response to injustice, it is not the way of Christ. The Gospel calls us to a higher standard—a standard of love that seeks the good of others, even our enemies. This does not mean being passive or silent in the face of evil. It means confronting evil with the truth and power of Christ, trusting that His love is stronger than hate and that His light can overcome any darkness.

The journey toward racial reconciliation is not an easy one. It requires courage, perseverance, and a willingness to step outside of our comfort zones. But it is a journey worth taking, for it is a journey that reflects the heart of God. It is a journey that leads us closer to the fulfillment of His Kingdom, where every tribe, tongue, and nation will worship together before His throne.

Let us never forget that the ultimate victory over racism and division has already been won through the cross of Christ. Our task is to live in light of that victory, proclaiming the good news of reconciliation until the day when every knee bows and every tongue confesses that Jesus Christ is Lord.

Chapter 8: "Living the Truth"

The journey toward dismantling the myth of race does not end with revelation—it begins there. For those who have embraced the truth of our shared humanity in Christ, the next step is to live it. This is not a passive endeavor but a radical, daily commitment to embody the principles of unity, justice, and love.

As the Apostle Paul urged, we must "work out [our] salvation with fear and trembling" (Philippians 2:12). This work transcends intellectual assent; it demands action rooted in divine conviction.

Years ago, during a sermon at my church in Newark, I posed a question to the congregation: "If we truly believe we are one in Christ, why do our lives so often reflect the divisions of the world?" The silence that followed was palpable. It is one thing to know the truth—it is another to let it reshape our relationships, priorities, and communities.

The answer to racial division is not merely theological—it is incarnational. Christ did not come to offer abstract ideals but to "dwell among us" (John 1:14). Likewise, our faith must move from the pew to the pavement. Consider the early church in Acts, where believers "had everything in common" (Acts 2:44). Their unity was not theoretical but economic, social, and sacrificial. They rejected the hierarchies of their day, whether Roman classism or Jewish exclusivity and modeled a countercultural community.

This is our blueprint. To live the truth, we must confront

the comfort of segregation—both physical and psychological. For me, this meant leaving the insulated suburbs to pastor in Newark's inner city. It meant hiring formerly incarcerated individuals not as charity but as equals. It meant sharing meals, resources, and stories with people whose life experiences differed radically from my own. Unity is costly. It requires us to relinquish the safety of sameness and step into the messiness of shared humanity.

The church, at its best, is a microcosm of God's kingdom—a place where "Jew and Gentile, slave and free" (Galatians 3:28) find common ground. Yet, too often, we have mirrored the world's divisions. I recall a conversation with a fellow pastor who dismissed my emphasis on multiethnic congregations, arguing, "People prefer to worship with their own kind." His words saddened me, for they revealed a surrender to the myth of race rather than a pursuit of Christ's vision.

True reconciliation begins when we redefine "our own kind." In Christ, our kinship is not determined by skin color but by spiritual rebirth. We partnered with predominantly white suburban churches at Bridge Builders Newark to fund job-training programs. Initially, skepticism ran high. Some of my Black congregants questioned whether these churches truly cared or were merely "checking a box."

Meanwhile, white volunteers often tiptoed around discussions of race, fearing offense. Yet barriers crumbled as we worked side by side—rebuilding homes, mentoring youth, and praying together. Relationships were formed over shared purpose, not performative allyship.

This is the church's role: to create spaces where grace

dismantles fear. It requires humility to listen, courage to repent, and faith to trust that God's Spirit can heal even the deepest wounds. When a white congregant tearfully apologized for his ancestors' role in slavery, and a Black mother forgave him, I witnessed the gospel in motion. Reconciliation is not a transaction—it is a transformation.

In Chapter 4, I introduced Shelby Steele's concept of the "anti-self"—the internalized narrative of inferiority that plagues many melanated individuals. But this anti-self also manifests collectively. It thrives in communities where systemic oppression has bred resignation, where generations have been told, "You are less than." Breaking this cycle demands more than individual resilience; it requires communal revival.

During a mentorship program at Bridge Builders, a young man named Jamal confessed, "I don't see the point. My dad's in jail, my mom's on drugs. I'm just waiting my turn." His despair mirrored the anti-self's lie: Your destiny is fixed. We surrounded Jamal with mentors—Black, white, Latino—who shared their own stories of overcoming. We connected him with job training and, crucially, affirmed his inherent worth. Today, Jamal oversees one of our construction crews, mentoring others trapped in the same cycle.

Communal healing happens when we replace the anti-self with the pro-self—the truth that we are "fearfully and wonderfully made" (Psalm 139:14). This requires systemic support: equitable education, economic investment, and advocacy. But it also demands spiritual defiance. When we teach our children their history—not just slavery and segregation but the resilience of Harriet Tubman, the brilliance of George Washington Carver, and the faith of Sojourner Truth—we arm them with a legacy of strength. We must be curators of hope. However, the ultimate lesson we must teach is that the God of all creation, created all men equal. You were created for a purpose, and that is not to be placed in a permanent place of submission and second class based on your skin color. But also that I am no better than the next man because of the "Color of my skin."

The issue of self-loathing versus superiority based on skin color runs deeper, much deeper than meets the eye. On self-loathing, for example, Carter G. Woodson reiterates a story of which he was personally privy to. Bear in mind that Woodson's book, from which I will quote, "The Miseducation of the Negro" was published in 1933. He states: A committee of Negros in a large city went to the owner of a chain store in their neighborhood and requested that they put a Negro Manager in charge. This man replied that he doubted that the Negros themselves wanted such a thing. The Negros urging him to make the change assured him that they were unanimously in favor of it. The manager, however, asked them to be fair enough with his firm and themselves to investigate before pressing the matter any further. They did so and discovered that 137 Negro families in that neighborhood seriously objected to buying from Negros and using articles handled by them. These Negros then had to do the groundwork of uprooting the inferiority idea which had resulted from their "Mis-Education."

[Miseducation pg. 161]

Now, on the opposite side, the unbalanced pendulum is

the narrative that "Blacks" are superior by virtue of the color of their skin. My jeremiad is that this is simply not true. Yah is the creator of all, and He is interested in one's character, not one's color! There remains much work to do. But I submit that the work should be done, that is, the correct re-education, not only of the Negro but of all mankind.

Racism is not America's sin alone—it is a global pandemic. From the caste systems of India to the tribal conflicts of Africa, the enemy's playbook is universal: divide and conquer. Yet so is God's answer. A pastor there told me, "Reconciliation is not forgetting. It is remembering—*together*—and choosing a new story."

This is our call. To the privileged: leverage your influence to dismantle inequity. To the oppressed: reject victimhood and reclaim your God-given agency to all. See beyond the narrow lens of race to the boundless image of God in every person.

The fight against racism is a marathon, not a sprint. There will be setbacks—laws repealed, hearts hardened, progress undone. Yet we run with hope.

Our task is to live as if God's truth is already realized. To vote, preach, teach, and labor in a way that prefigures the coming Kingdom. This is not naivety—it is prophecy in action. As Dr. King proclaimed, "The arc of the moral universe is long, but it bends toward justice." It bends because the hands of the faithful bend it.

Let us be those hands. Let us be the ones who, in the words of Isaiah, "repair the broken walls" (Isaiah 58:12) of division. The myth of race has no power over those who walk in the light of truth. We are not Black, white, or brown—we are Christ's. And in Him, we are free.

"Now the Lord is the Spirit, and where the Spirit of the Lord is, there is freedom."

—2 Corinthians 3:17

Truth is not merely something to be acknowledged; it must be lived, breathed, and carried into the spaces where falsehood has long reigned. It is one thing to intellectually reject the myth of race; it is another to walk daily in the freedom of Christ's vision for humanity. This journey requires both courage and conviction.

As I reflect on my own walk, I am reminded of the costs of truth-telling. There were seasons when I faced rejection— even from within the church. When I first began preaching on racial reconciliation, some congregants grew uneasy. One family left, saying I was "bringing politics into the pulpit." Another well-meaning elder advised me to focus on "spiritual matters" rather than social issues. But how could I? Jesus did not merely preach about the soul; He healed the sick, fed the hungry, and upended systems of injustice. His gospel was not escapism—it was incarnation.

One Sunday, a middle-aged Black woman approached me after delivering a sermon on breaking down racial barriers. Tears welled in her eyes as she whispered, "Pastor, I've been waiting to hear this from the pulpit my whole life."

Her words struck me deeply. How many had waited in silence, longing for the church to be more than a sanctuary from injustice—but an instrument against it? How many had sat in pews where calls for justice were labeled "divisive" rather than biblical? Living the truth means speaking it, even when it is uncomfortable.

Yet, the truth does not merely dismantle—it rebuilds. I have witnessed transformation where it once seemed impossible. Rich, a dear friend of mine, informed me during a round of golf about an organization that provided summer camp opportunities to kids from Newark. Newark is a big city (as New Jersey goes) of about 290,000 people. So, I had never heard of this organization. I was intrigued as Rich told me about how this organization was run by believers on a shoestring budget. He let me know that they had several needs on their campus, including sheds that needed to be built, roofs that needed repair, and rooms that needed to be remodeled.

Several months later, I met the proprietors of the organization at their annual golf outing, which I was happy to support. After speaking with the founders, I knew we had to help. So, I marshalled our staff at Bridge Builders to go to their campus for a "Day of Giving." We brought up a full crew with all of our carpentry tools and materials. We built a partial roof, repaired a roof, and built a shed – pro bono. Needless to say, they were quite grateful. Now, let me fill in some blanks. The owners of the organization are "white," Rich is "white," I am "black," and all of my staff are "black" and "brown." Never did "Color" figure into this transaction as it should and could be. I give you this example of a colorless collaboration. We can work together and produce position outcomes without prejudice.

The call to live the truth extends beyond personal relationships—it demands systemic change. Racial reconciliation is not merely about sentiment; it requires structure. The early church did not merely affirm unity; they practiced it in tangible ways—redistributing wealth, caring for widows, and challenging injustice.

One of the most difficult truths I have had to face is that good intentions are not enough. Charity is not the same as justice. I learned this firsthand while working with Bridge Builders Newark. In the early years, well-meaning volunteers would come, paint houses, and leave feeling accomplished. Yet, nothing changed for the residents. We had to shift from temporary aid to long-term investment— job creation, affordable housing, and leadership development. Living the truth means ensuring that justice is not an occasional act but a permanent reality.

Perhaps one of the greatest challenges of our time is raising children who are not burdened by the divisions we inherited. I often think of my own children and the world they will navigate.

Parents, educators, and church leaders have a sacred duty to shape the next generation in truth. This means telling the full history—not just of pain, but of perseverance. It means teaching children to recognize injustice, not as an abstract concept but as something they are called to resist. It means showing them that unity is not passive—it is built with hands and hearts willing to labor for it.

One summer, during a youth leadership camp, a Black teenage boy hesitated before shaking the hand of a white mentor. "My dad told me never to trust them," he admitted. Rather than taking offense, the mentor responded, "Then let me earn it." And he did. Over weeks of mentorship, that young man's perspective shifted—not because of a lecture, but because he saw, in action, what reconciliation looked like.

Living the truth requires more than acknowledgment—it demands movement. We must:

- ➤ *Disrupt our comfort zones.* Attend churches, schools, and communities that reflect God's diverse kingdom—not just our preferences.

- ➤ *Invest in justice.* Support policies that promote equity, not just charity.

- ➤ *Be bridge-builders.* Engage in honest conversations, even when they are difficult.

- ➤ *Model kingdom culture.* Let our homes, workplaces, and ministries reflect the values of unity and dignity.

The world will not be transformed by passive agreement but by radical obedience. As Jesus declared, "You will know the truth, and the truth will set you free" (John 8:32).

The myth of race can only be dismantled by those willing to live in the freedom of God's truth. The time is now. Let us walk in it.

Chapter 9: Origins and Identity

When I think about the origins of mankind and the diversity of skin tones, I find myself returning to one powerful narrative—the story of Noah and his sons. It's a story that has been passed down for generations, a part of the Torah narrative that has shaped not just religious thought but our collective understanding of who we are as mankind. As I've delved deeper into this story, I've come to realize just how much it offers us in terms of understanding the shared origins of all people, no matter the color of their skin.

The story of Noah and his three sons—Shem, Ham, and Japheth—holds profound significance. After the great flood, Noah and his family emerged as the sole survivors of a world that had been wiped clean of its former sins. This small family would be the progenitors who would repopulate the earth. Each of Noah's sons is believed to be the ancestor of different groups of people, with Shem often regarded as the ancestor of the Semitic peoples, Ham as the father of the African nations, and Japheth as the progenitor of many European and Asian nations. This biblical account has been used over the centuries to explain the origin of the world's peoples and, unfortunately, the differences in skin tones.

For a long time, I accepted this story as a way to explain the diversity of mankind. But as I've learned more, I've come to realize just how important it is to understand what this narrative truly represents—and what it doesn't. There's a fundamental truth that's often lost in the retelling of this story: all people, regardless of where they come from or the color of their skin, trace their lineage back to the same source. We are all descendants of Noah. We are one family united by a shared heritage. This fact is vital to understand as we move forward in challenging harmful myths about race and skin color.

Challenging the Myths About Skin Color and Value

I've often encountered harmful ideas about race and skin color—ideas that suggest that one group of people is inherently superior or inferior to another based on the color of their skin. These myths are deeply ingrained in society and have been used to justify some of mankind's darkest moments, from slavery to segregation to genocide. It's easy to see how these misconceptions could arise, but when I reflect on the story of Noah and his sons, I can't help but be struck by the overwhelming truth that these divisions are based on falsehoods.

Skin color is simply a physical characteristic shaped by thousands of years of adaptation to various environments. I've learned that darker skin, for example, is an adaptation to the intense sunlight near the equator, while lighter skin developed in regions with less sunlight as a way to absorb more vitamin D. These differences are rooted in our biology and environment, not in inherent differences in value or ability. Yet, throughout history, people have used these differences to create unjust hierarchies—associating skin color with everything from intelligence to morality to worth.

The story of Noah's sons doesn't support any of these myths. In fact, it's quite the opposite. It reminds me that all of humanity shares a common ancestry. We're all part of the same family—no one group is superior to another. In God's eyes, we are all equally valuable. The message of the Torah is clear: we are all made in the image of Yah (God), and that image transcends any external differences, including the color of our skin.

The Beauty of Unity in Diversity

One of the most profound lessons I've learned from the story of Noah's descendants is the beauty of unity in diversity. Noah's three sons became the ancestors of distinct nations, cultures, and peoples, each with their unique traditions, languages, and customs. These differences, however, don't mean that one group is better or worse than another—they are a reflection of the richness and complexity of mankind's experience. We can celebrate these differences without resorting to division.

I've come to appreciate the fact that diversity is not something to fear or judge but something to embrace. The different skin tones we see in the world today are a testament to mankind's adaptability and creativity. They speak to the history of migration, exploration, and settlement in different parts of the world. The wide range of human features, from hair texture to eye shape to skin color, reflects the wonder of human evolution and the resilience of the spirit of mankind.

The more I reflect on this, the more I see that the true story of mankind is one of connection, not division. We are all part of the same earthly family, and our differences should not create barriers between us. Instead, they should be a cause for celebration, a reminder of the incredible variety of experiences and backgrounds that make up the world we live in.

Embracing a Shared Identity

The more I study the origins of humanity and the story of Noah's descendants, the more I realize the importance of embracing a shared identity. No matter where we come from or what our skin looks like, we are all part of the same family. This truth is crucial in today's world, where racism and division still persist in many forms. We have to challenge the notion that one group of people is more valuable than another based on their "race" or ethnicity.

I believe it is essential for us to see beyond the surface and recognize that, at our core, we are all joined because we share the same progenitor. I know this may be shocking to you and may be the cause for some cognitive dissonance, but let truth challenge you and perhaps reset the values of your long-held belief systems, particularly when it comes to falsely formed ideology surrounding so-called "race." We share the same fundamental desires for love, peace, and belonging. We all have the capacity for kindness, compassion, and growth. When I think about my own interactions with people from different backgrounds, I realize how much I have learned from them and how much our shared origin connects us. It's through this understanding that we can begin to break down the barriers that divide us and build a world where every person is treated with the dignity and respect they deserve.

Conclusion: The Shared Human Experience

Looking back on the story of Noah's sons, I am reminded of the importance of unity in our shared origin. We all trace our roots back to the same family, regardless of skin color or cultural background. This understanding is not just important for historical or religious reasons—it's vital for how we interact with one another in the world today.

The myths that tie skin color to value or inherent differences have no place in the world I want to live in. As I reflect on the story of Noah's descendants, I'm reminded that the true message is one of love, equality, and shared identity. All people, regardless of where they come from, are equally valuable and deserving of respect.

As we move forward in a world that is increasingly diverse, let us remember that we are all part of the same family, united by our shared origins. When we embrace this truth, we can build a more compassionate and just world where the beauty of our diversity is celebrated, not feared.

Migration, Climate, and Adaptation: Natural Causes for Physical Variations

As I explore the variations in skin tone and hair texture across humanity, *I come to understand that these differences are the result of natural processes shaped by the environment rather than an indicator of inherent value or worth.* Migration, climate, and adaptation are the driving forces behind the diversity we see in the physical characteristics of people today.

The human race, despite its vast differences in appearance, all share the same origin. Our ancestors originally lived in Africa, and as populations migrated across the globe, they adapted to new climates and environments. The color of our skin, for example, is primarily determined by the amount of melanin in our bodies, which is a protective response to sunlight. The closer a population lived to the equator, the more melanin they developed to shield their skin from the harmful effects of ultraviolet (UV) rays. This explains why people from regions with intense sunlight, like sub-Saharan Africa, generally have darker skin, as it provides them with protection against sunburn and skin cancers.

Conversely, as humans migrated to regions with less sunlight, such as Northern Europe, there was a genetic shift toward lighter skin. In these regions, the need for melanin decreased, and lighter skin allowed for more efficient absorption of the scarce UV rays, which are essential for producing vitamin D in the body. The variation in hair texture, too, can be attributed to the climate. People in warmer, tropical regions often have tightly coiled hair, which is believed to offer protection against excessive heat by providing ventilation to the scalp. In colder climates, straight or wavy hair was more advantageous as it helped to preserve body heat.

This process of adaptation and migration has given rise to the wide range of physical traits we see in the world today. But it's important to understand that these differences are not indicative of the superiority or inferiority of one group over another. Instead, they are simply the result of humans adapting to their environments over millennia. Physical features such as skin tone and hair texture are superficial in nature and have no bearing on a person's worth or capabilities.

The True Identity of Mankind: Not in Racial Categories, But in a Shared Origin and Purpose

When I reflect on mankind's physical diversity, I am reminded that our true identity lies not in racial categories but in our shared origin and common purpose. From a biological perspective, all human beings belong to the same species—Homo sapiens. This means that regardless of skin color, hair texture, or facial features, we are all fundamentally the same. Our differences are superficial and should not be used to categorize or divide us.

Our shared origin stems from the understanding that all humans are descendants of the same ancestral line. From a religious perspective, many traditions, including the story of Noah's descendants in the Bible, tell us that we all come from a common family. This idea reinforces the notion that, at our core, we are all part of the same–family, and any division based on physical appearance is artificial.

At a deeper level, our true identity also lies in our shared purpose as mankind. Regardless of where we come from, we all seek love, belonging, and meaning in our lives. We share similar dreams, fears, and aspirations. We all strive for connection, and we all have the capacity for kindness, empathy, and growth. The diversity of humanity, when viewed through the lens of our shared identity, is not something that separates us but something that enriches our collective experience.

Our common purpose transcends "race" and ethnicity. We are all tasked with the responsibility of contributing to the well-being of our families, communities, and the world at large. Whether we are working toward personal growth or addressing global challenges such as poverty, climate change, or social justice, our shared quest for well-being unites us in our mission to make the world a better place. Our true identity is not determined by the superficial differences we perceive but by our collective ability to love, learn, and contribute to the common good.

Theme: Mankind's Differences Are Superficial; Unity Lies in Understanding Our Shared Origins

The theme of this discussion is simple yet profound: mankind's differences are superficial, and our unity lies in understanding our shared origins. The physical traits that differentiate us—skin tone, hair texture, facial features—are merely the result of natural adaptation to different environments. These differences are not a reflection of our worth or capabilities but are part of the vast spectrum of human diversity shaped by thousands of years of migration and environmental change.

When I consider the world's many cultures, languages, and traditions, it becomes clear that these differences are not barriers but rather expressions of the richness of human experience. We may have different customs, foods, and ways of life, but these differences should not be a source of division. Instead, they should be a reminder of the beauty and resilience of the spirit of mankind. In the grand scheme of history, we are all descendants of the same family, and our shared origin binds us together.

Understanding our shared origins allows us to see beyond physical appearance and cultural differences, helping us to embrace one another as equals. It shifts our focus from superficial distinctions to a deeper appreciation for the common humanity that unites us all. It reminds us that no matter where we come from or how we look, we are all part of the same family with the same hopes, dreams, and capacity for love.

Key Takeaway: Embracing a Shared Identity Dismantles the Power of Racial Divisions

The key takeaway here is that embracing our shared identity is the key to dismantling the power of racial divisions. By recognizing that our differences in skin tone, hair texture, and other physical features are the result of natural adaptation, we can begin to reject the myths that have been used to justify inequality and injustice. These divisions—based on race, ethnicity, or appearance—are arbitrary and have no bearing on our inherent worth as human beings.

When we embrace our shared humanity, we open ourselves up to deeper connections with one another. We recognize that the things that make us different are not sources of division but opportunities for growth and learning. We can appreciate and celebrate the diversity of cultures, traditions, and experiences without seeing them as barriers to understanding. By doing so, we create a world where racial divisions no longer have power over our relationships, our opportunities, or our sense of community.

Ultimately, our true identity lies not in the color of our skin or the texture of our hair but in the shared origin we all have and the collective purpose we pursue as human beings. It is in this understanding that we find the strength to overcome prejudice, discrimination, and division. By embracing our shared identity, we can work together to build a more just, compassionate, and united world.

Chapter 10: The Tower of Babel and Language

Language is one of mankind's most powerful tools. It can build bridges, create barriers, foster understanding, or fuel division. Throughout history, language has shaped civilizations, guided cultural development, and even determined power dynamics between people and groups. But long before linguistic diversity became a defining feature of human society, the origins of division through language can be traced back to a pivotal moment in Torah history—the account of the Tower of Babel.

The Story of Babel: The First Great Division

The account of the Tower of Babel in Genesis 11 tells of a time when all people spoke a single language and worked together in unity. Their goal was to build a city with a tower reaching the heavens, a monument to their own greatness. This was not merely an architectural endeavor; it was an act of defiance against Yah's sovereignty. Their intention was not just to create something magnificent but to assert their own independence from God.

Seeing the pride and ambition of man, Yah intervened. Rather than destroying them outright, He confounded their speech, causing them to speak in different languages. Unable to communicate effectively, they abandoned their project and scattered across the earth. The division of language marked the beginning of distinct people groups, each developing its own culture and identity. This biblical account presents language not only as a divine gift but also as a means of humbling man when unity is sought for the wrong reasons.

The lesson from Babel is clear: unity without righteousness leads to arrogance, and when communication is used to serve self-interest rather than divine purpose, division inevitably follows. The scattering of the people across the earth was not just a punishment but also a redirection—a way to ensure that man would not fall victim to unchecked pride.

Language as the First Major Tool of Division

The fragmentation of language at Babel was the first recorded instance of communication becoming a dividing force among people. Since then, language has continued to serve as both a barrier and a means of control. Throughout history, linguistic differences have been used to foster misunderstandings, create social hierarchies, and reinforce divisions among people and groups.

Consider how colonial empires imposed their languages on indigenous populations, often erasing native tongues and, with them, cultural identities. In many countries, language has been a marker of privilege—those who speak the dominant tongue fluently gain access to education, political influence, and economic opportunities, while those who do not are marginalized. Even within a single language, dialects and accents can create divisions, signaling social class, ethnicity, or geographical origin.

For example, in the United States, African American Vernacular English (AAVE) has long been stigmatized as "improper" English despite being a linguistically rich and rule-governed dialect. This linguistic prejudice has contributed to systemic discrimination in education and employment, reinforcing racial disparities. Similarly, in many parts of the world, indigenous languages have been suppressed in favor of colonial languages, leading to the gradual erosion of cultural heritage and identity.

Racial and societal divisions have often been reinforced by language, as seen in segregation-era America, where African Americans were often deemed 'uneducated' or 'less intelligent' based on their dialects. The same prejudices have been applied to immigrants who speak English as a second language, limiting their opportunities and reinforcing cultural divisions. Miscommunication and linguistic biases have historically fueled societal and racial divisions, perpetuating misunderstandings and systemic inequalities.

The Modern-Day Babel: How Language Fuels Societal and Racial Divisions

In today's world, we continue to see how language serves as a battleground for identity and power. The rhetoric used in political discourse, media, and education shapes perceptions of race, class, and belonging. Terms like "illegal immigrant," "inner-city communities," or "articulate" when used to describe a person of color carry layers of coded meaning, often perpetuating stereotypes and biases.

Social media and digital communication have only amplified this effect. While these platforms enable global connection, they also create echo chambers where language is manipulated to divide rather than unite. Words are weaponized, and the way issues are framed determines whether they bring people together or deepen divisions. The misuse of communication and the lack of mutual understanding have contributed to growing tensions between different racial and social groups.

Political leaders, media outlets, and cultural influencers wield language to shape public perception, often using it as a tool of manipulation. For example, framing a protest as a "riot" versus a "demonstration" carries significant implications for how the event is perceived. Similarly, the language used to describe different groups of people—whether refugees, migrants, or expatriates—can dictate levels of empathy and acceptance.

Language as a Tool for Reconciliation and Unity

If language was once a tool for division, it can also be reclaimed as a tool for unity. Just as Yah (God) used language at Babel to scatter people, He later used language to reunite them. In the New Testament, the Day of Pentecost (Acts 2) serves as a powerful counterpoint to Babel. As the Holy Spirit descended upon Jesus' disciples, they began speaking in different tongues, enabling people from various nations to understand them. Unlike Babel, where language was divided, Pentecost demonstrated how divine intervention could use language to foster understanding and unity.

In our own time, we have the opportunity to use language to bridge divides rather than widen them. This begins with awareness—recognizing how language shapes our perceptions and being intentional in how we speak about others. It requires us to challenge stereotypes, reject divisive rhetoric, and choose words that promote inclusivity and understanding.

Moreover, we must listen. True reconciliation comes

not just from speaking the right words but from genuinely hearing others. By engaging with diverse perspectives and valuing different linguistic and cultural expressions, we can break down barriers and build relationships based on mutual respect.

One inspiring example of language being used for reconciliation is the Truth and Reconciliation Commission (TRC) in South Africa. After the end of apartheid, the TRC provided a platform where victims and perpetrators could share their experiences in their own words. By allowing individuals to speak and be heard in a meaningful way, the TRC played a crucial role in national healing. This demonstrates the power of language not just as a means of communication but as a pathway to understanding and transformation.

The Key to Healing: Intentional Connection and Communication

The story of Babel reminds us that division often begins with misunderstanding, but it does not have to end there. While language has historically been used to separate and categorize people, it also has the power to heal, unify, and elevate shared truths. When wielded with wisdom, humility, and love, words become a means of reconciliation rather than conflict.

As we navigate a world still plagued by racial and societal divisions, let us remember that our words matter. We can choose to use language to affirm one another's humanity rather than diminish it. By embracing intentional connection, thoughtful dialogue, and compassionate communication, we move one step closer to the unity that was lost at Babel—but that can still be reclaimed today.

The challenge before us is not simply to recognize the role of language in division but to take active steps toward using it as a force for unity. This requires patience, effort, and a willingness to engage with those who may think and speak differently. It calls us to move beyond surface-level interactions and into deep, meaningful conversations that foster mutual respect and genuine understanding.

Key Takeaway: Bridging Gaps in Understanding is a Path to Healing and Unity

The story of the Tower of Babel illustrates how misunderstanding and miscommunication can lead to fragmentation, while the Day of Pentecost shows that language, when guided by wisdom and purpose, can bring people together. Throughout history, language has been a powerful tool—both for division and reconciliation. Societal and racial divides have been fueled by linguistic differences, from colonial language suppression to modern rhetoric shaping public perception.

Yet, as the chapter explores, language can also be reclaimed as a means of unity. By challenging divisive rhetoric, fostering intentional dialogue, and actively listening to diverse voices, we can transform language into a bridge rather than a barrier. Whether in political discourse, education, or everyday conversations, choosing words that heal rather than harm is essential for overcoming the deep-rooted divisions that persist in society.

Healing begins with intentional connection. When we recognize language as a tool for both power and restoration, we can dismantle historical prejudices and create spaces where all voices are heard and valued. True unity does not come from erasing differences, but from understanding them—by communicating with empathy, respect, and a commitment to truth, we take a vital step toward reconciliation and collective progress.

Chapter 11: Race in Scripture – A Book of Character

Historically, individuals have exploited scripture to legitimize different social hierarchies, including racial classifications that encourage discrimination and separation. The Bible, when approached sincerely and with awareness of its cultural and historical background, does not endorse any hierarchies founded on race (remember the very concept of "race" is a man-made construct), ethnicity, or skin tone. Rather, it highlights the significance of character, conduct, and the inner traits that define an individual. In this chapter, we will examine how scripture has been misunderstood concerning race and demonstrate that the genuine message of the Torah and Tanach, aka The Bible, advocates for unity, love, and respect for everyone, no matter their skin tone or ethnic origins.

The Misuse of Scripture to Justify Racial Hierarchies

A major challenge in comprehending race in scripture is the historical abuse of the Bible by individuals aiming to legitimize racial hierarchies. Throughout different eras in history, people and groups have understood specific passages in ways that upheld the concept of racial dominance and subordination. For instance, in the period of slavery in the United States, certain slave owners and advocates of slavery referenced the curse of Ham from the Old Testament (Genesis 9:18-27) to support the claim that black individuals were meant to be servants. They contended that Noah's curse on Ham's offspring legitimized the oppression of African individuals.

Nonetheless, this understanding is both inaccurate and detrimental. The account of Noah and his sons in Genesis does not refer to race or skin tone. The curse is aimed not at Ham himself but rather at his son, Canaan, and it does not suggest any intrinsic disparity in value or respect among various ethnicities. Instead, the curse pronounced was due to a massive defect of perversion in the soul of Ham (again, not the color of his skin). For centuries, this excerpt was employed to justify the oppression and abuse of African individuals, illustrating how religious texts can be distorted to support a detrimental purpose.

Likewise, during colonial periods, European colonizers frequently referenced biblical doctrines to rationalize their control over indigenous populations and other ethnic groups. The concept of Europeans' "divine right" to dominate others was frequently associated with religious texts, bolstering a belief in racial superiority that has caused enduring damage to societies globally.

The inappropriate use of scripture is not confined to earlier generations. Even now, some individuals and groups continue to utilize biblical scriptures to support racist beliefs. Yet, an in-depth and precise interpretation of scripture uncovers a distinct message—one that upholds the equality and worth of every individual, irrespective of their skin tone or ethnicity.

The Bible's Emphasis on Character and Behavior

Upon closer examination of the Bible, it is apparent that Scripture consistently emphasizes character and conduct over external traits such as skin color. The main message of the Bible is not focused on someone's skin color or ethnicity but rather on the individual's character, their treatment of others, and how they practice their beliefs.

One of the clearest expressions of this emphasis on character comes from the teachings of Jesus Christ. In Matthew 7:16-20, Jesus tells his followers, "By their fruit, you will recognize them." He is not speaking about the outward appearance of a person but rather their deeds and actions. It is the fruit—what a person produces through their actions and behavior—that matters, not their external characteristics.

Throughout his ministry, Jesus continually defied the racial and ethnic boundaries that society of his time sought to impose. He reached out to Samaritans, who many Jews despised, and he healed Gentiles, showing that God's love is not limited to one particular person or group. In the parable of the Good Samaritan (Luke 10:25-37), Jesus turned the expectations of his Jewish audience upside down by making a Samaritan—the very people the Jews often considered inferior—the hero of the story. This was a powerful statement about the kind of character that pleases God: compassion, mercy, and love for one's neighbor, regardless of racial or ethnic background.

The Apostle Paul echoes this teaching throughout his letters. In Galatians 3:28, he writes, "There is neither Jew nor Greek, slave nor free, male nor female, for you are all one in Christ Jesus." This statement radically challenges any attempt to divide people based on skin color, class, or gender. Paul emphasizes that in Christ, all distinctions are erased, and what matters is the shared identity as children of

Yah the Most High. In the same way, he calls on Believers to live out this unity by treating one another with love and respect, regardless of their background.

Another example can be found in the book of James. In James 2:1-9, James addresses the sin of favoritism, warning believers not to show partiality based on wealth, social status, or external appearances. He writes, "If you show favoritism, you sin and are convicted by the law as lawbreakers." This teaching applies not only to favoritism based on wealth but also to any form of prejudice, including racial bias. James calls for a church community that is characterized by equality and love, where all people are valued based on their character, not their external appearance.

The Universal Call to Love and Respect All People

One of the Bible's most consistent themes is the call to love one's neighbor. In Matthew 22:37-39, when Jesus is asked about the greatest commandment, he responds by summarizing the entire law: "Love the Lord your God with all your heart, with all your soul, and with all your mind. This is the first and greatest commandment. And the second is like it: Love your neighbor as yourself." Jesus makes no distinctions here about who qualifies as a neighbor. The command to love extends to everyone, regardless of race, ethnicity, or background.

This message is reinforced throughout the Bible. In Leviticus 19:18, the Israelites are commanded to "love your neighbor as yourself," a principle that is affirmed by Jesus and his apostles. The Bible repeatedly emphasizes that love for others is not conditional upon their race, social standing, or nationality. Instead, it is based on a shared human dignity and the understanding that all people are created in the image of our Father (Genesis 1:26-27).

In the parable of the Good Samaritan, Jesus teaches that loving one's neighbor goes beyond ethnic or cultural boundaries. The Samaritan, who is considered an outsider by the Jews, demonstrates true love and compassion by helping a man in need, while the priest and Levite—members of the same religious community as the injured man—pass by without offering assistance. Jesus concludes the parable by saying, "Go and do likewise" (Luke 10:37), urging his followers to show love and mercy to all people, regardless of their skin tone or background.

Key Biblical Figures: People of Color in Scripture

In challenging the Westernized portrayal of biblical figures, it's important to highlight key figures such as **Moses**, **David**, and **Abraham**, who were all people of color, reflecting the diverse ethnic backgrounds of the ancient world.

- **Moses**: Often depicted as a Western figure in modern portrayals, Moses was born in Egypt, a multicultural society in northeastern Africa. He was raised in Pharaoh's court, which had a mixed population. Moses himself would have likely shared the physical traits common among Egyptians and other peoples in that region, suggesting he was a person of color. His marriage to Zipporah, a Midianite woman, further emphasizes the diversity of his life and ministry, underscoring his connection to various ethnic groups.

- **David**: King David, while often depicted through a Europeanized lens, came from a region that was home to numerous ethnic groups, including the Israelites, Philistines, and Canaanites. His story, particularly his interactions with various people groups, shows that his identity was tied to the cultural melting pot of the ancient Near East. Furthermore, David's line, which includes Jesus Christ, demonstrates that his faith, not his ethnicity, was what mattered most in God's eyes.

- **Abraham**: The father of many nations, Abraham was born in Ur (modern-day Iraq), a region known for its ethnic and cultural diversity. His background challenges any simplistic racial interpretation, as Ur was a hub of various peoples, including Sumerians and Akkadians. God's covenant with Abraham was not based on his ethnicity but on his faith, demonstrating that God's promises transcend racial boundaries.

These examples of biblical figures reveal that the people central to God's plan were part of a complex, multicultural world. Their faith, obedience, and actions—not their "race"—were what made them central to Yahovah's purposes.

Yah Does Not Define Humanity by Race but by Faith, Obedience, and Actions

The Bible consistently demonstrates that Yah does not prioritize race or ethnicity but instead values faith, obedience, and moral character.

- **Faith and Obedience Over Skin Color**: Throughout the Bible, God's approval of individuals is based on their trust in Him and their willingness to follow His commands. For instance, Abraham is revered not for the color of his skin or ethnic background but for his obedience and faith in Yah's promises (Genesis 12:1-3). Similarly, the great figures of Israel, including Moses and David, are honored for their faith and adherence to Yah's will.

- **The Inclusivity of God's Kingdom**: Yeshuah's (Jesus') ministry, particularly His interactions with non-Jews, exemplifies that race is not a determining factor in God's kingdom. He reached out to Samaritans, Romans, and Gentiles, challenging societal norms and breaking down ethnic barriers. The Apostle Paul further emphasizes this in Galatians 3:28, stating, "There is neither Jew nor Greek, slave nor free, male nor female, for you are all one in Christ Jesus." In this new community, race and other distinctions are irrelevant, and the focus is on one's faith and actions in Christ.

This theme reinforces that Yah's judgment and view of humanity are not shaped by external appearances but by an individual's faithfulness, love, and actions. Yah's call is to live in unity, serving and loving one another regardless of racial or ethnic differences.

Theme: Scripture Speaks to the Character and Purpose of Humanity, Not Racial Divisions

The central message of scripture revolves around the character and purpose of humanity. God's plan is to redeem all of humanity, and this plan is not confined to any specific "race," ethnicity, or nationality. Rather, the Bible speaks to the way people live, the choices they make, and how they align their lives with His will. This emphasis on character over race is pivotal in understanding Scripture's broader message.

- **The Role of Faith**: The Bible consistently highlights the importance of faith. From the faith of Abraham to the teachings of Jesus and the apostles, faith is the key to a relationship with God. This faith transcends ethnic divisions and invites people of all backgrounds into Elohim's redemptive plan.

- **The Call to Love and Unity**: Jesus calls His followers to love one another, regardless of race or background. In John 13:34-35, He commands His disciples to love each other as He has loved them, for this is the way the world will know they are His followers. The Bible teaches that love and unity are the foundation of the Believer's community, not racial or ethnic homogeneity.

Thus, scripture does not promote racial division but rather speaks to humanity's shared purpose—to love Yah and others, to live faithfully, and to pursue justice and righteousness, all of which transcend any skin color or ethnic barriers.

Key Takeaway: Misinterpretations of Scripture Have Caused Harm, But Its Truth Reveals Unity and Shared Value in Yehovah's Eyes

Throughout history, misinterpretations of scripture have led to harm, particularly in perpetuating racist ideologies and justifying discrimination. The misuse of passages like the Curse of Ham or selective readings of Paul's letters has often been used to enforce racial hierarchies. However, a proper understanding of scripture reveals that these interpretations are not reflective of God's true message.

- **Unity in Christ**: The key takeaway is that the Bible's true message is one of unity and equality. God does not define humanity by race but by faith, character, and actions. The figures of Moses, David, Abraham, and others were valued by God not for their race but for their faithfulness and obedience. The New Testament, particularly the writings of Paul and the teachings of Jesus, calls believers to love all people equally, regardless of their background.

- **The Truth of Scripture**: When we understand Scripture through its correct context, we see that God's plan is to unite people of all races and ethnicities in Christ. There is no distinction in God's eyes between Jew or Gentile, slave or free, male or female. In Christ, all people are equal, and the focus is on living in accordance with Yah's will.

Thus, the truth of scripture calls for a rejection of racial divisions and an embrace of unity, love, and mutual respect. By highlighting the faith, obedience, and actions of biblical figures, we see that what God values in humanity is not skin color or ethnicity but the righteousness of soul, heart, and character.

Chapter 12: Approaching an Answer

Joe Madison once likened racism to a virus—a relentless, mutating force that adapts to survive even as societies evolve. Like a pathogen, it infiltrates institutions, poisons relationships, and resists eradication through superficial treatments.

Mankind has suffered from this disease for ages, yet it still exists today, evolving from overt segregation into structural injustices, microaggressions, and intolerance in the digital age. The issue we need to address is not just how racism persists but also why it is so deeply ingrained in our society after decades of political activism, legal challenges, and social advancement.

Affirmative action programs and the Civil Rights Act are two examples of legislative breakthroughs that have opened doors previously closed by discrimination and demolished overt barriers. Social campaigns have contested stereotypes, and political activism has given voice to the voiceless. DE &I (Diversity, Equity, and Inclusion) initiatives have been championed. Albeit, at the time of this writing, many of these policies are being repealed in the United States. However, despite their admirable intentions, these initiatives have fallen short. While laws can control conduct, they cannot change people's hearts. As one American President put it, "You can not legislate righteousness."

Although education can enlighten people, it cannot eliminate deeply rooted prejudices. Although they can redistribute wealth, economic changes cannot mend the rifts caused by mistrust between people groups.

The failure of these solutions lies in their focus on symptoms rather than the disease itself. Racism is not merely a social ill or political defect; it is a spiritual malignancy. It thrives in the soil of humanity's fallen nature—a nature corrupted by sin, pride, and the innate inclination to elevate oneself above others.

As the prophet Jeremiah declared, "The heart is deceitful above all things and beyond cure. Who can understand it?" (Jeremiah 17:9).

No policy can purify a heart that clings to superiority. No protest can heal a soul that fears difference.

The Spiritual Roots of Division

Fundamentally, racism is an act of disobedience to the divine order. Each and every person has equal dignity because, as Genesis teaches, we were made in God's image and likeness (Genesis 1:27). However, this oneness was shattered by the Fall. The ambition to rule others is fueled by the same ego that led Adam and Eve to believe they were gods. A warning that unity can become an instrument of oppression when it is separated from righteousness is echoed throughout history by the Tower of Babel, where language was jumbled to humble human arrogance.

The apostle Paul referred to our fallen nature as "the flesh"—the self-centered, immoral tendencies that sow discord, fear, and wrath (Galatians 5:19–21). One of the fruits of this tainted tree is racism. Because its roots are in a condition that no legislator can vote away—the brokenness of the human heart—it cannot be eliminated by human effort alone.

Racism requires a spiritual answer if it is a spiritual issue. Recognizing our shared desire for atonement is the first step in finding the solution.

"For all have sinned and fall short of the glory of God" (Romans 3:23). No one is immune to the taint of prejudice, whether overt or unconscious. Healing starts when we confess this truth and turn to the only power capable of renewing our hearts: the transformative love of Christ.

Jesus' ministry modeled this radical renewal. He dismantled ethnic barriers, honoring the faith of a Roman centurion (Matthew 8:5-13), saving a Samaritan woman (John 4:1-42), and praising a Canaanite mother's persistence (Matthew 15:21-28). His death on the cross tore down the "dividing wall of hostility" between peoples (Ephesians 2:14), offering reconciliation not just to God but to one another. This is the Gospel's power: it does not whitewash differences but redeems them, weaving diverse threads into a tapestry of divine grace.

The Apostle Paul called love "the most excellent way" (1 Corinthians 12:31). It is the antidote to fear, the balm for hatred, and the engine of justice. Christ's command to "love your neighbor as yourself" (Matthew 22:39) is not a sentimental ideal but a revolutionary mandate. Love compels us to listen before judging, to serve rather than dominate, and to see God's image in those society deems "other."

This love comes from the Holy Spirit, who "pours out God's love into our hearts" (Romans 5:5); it is not self-generated. Believers are prepared to face their prejudices, confess their culpability, and actively destroy oppressive institutions via prayer, scripture, and community. This is the work of Bridge Builders Newark (our for-profit construction firm discussed earlier), a company that demonstrates how divine love drives both individual salvation and social development by combining spiritual mentoring with hands-on job training.

A Call to Divine Intervention

Even with the best of intentions, man-made methods are unable to treat a spiritual illness. Racism deserves supernatural intervention, just as a virus requires a vaccine. While acknowledging their limits, this does not discount the importance of activism, education, or policy. Allowing God to rebuild our hearts and refocus our priorities is the first step toward true healing.

Promise of The Revelation 7:9—a vision of "every nation, tribe, people, and language" united in worship—offers hope despite the difficult path ahead. We are commanded to live as forerunners of this kingdom until that time, repairing damaged walls and restoring streets so that people can live there (Isaiah 58:12).

Key Takeaway

Racism is a mirror reflecting humanity's fallen state, and no human strategy can fully erase its stain. The solution lies beyond us—in the transformative power of faith, the relentless pursuit of love, and the spiritual renewal only Christ can bring. As we embrace this truth, we move from despair to hope, knowing that "where the Spirit of the Lord is, there is freedom" (2 Corinthians 3:17). The journey toward racial reconciliation is not a political campaign but a pilgrimage of the heart, guided by the One who makes all things new.

Chapter 13: Love as the Answer

Racism, as we have explored, is a spiritual malignancy rooted in humanity's fallen nature. No policy, protest, or program can fully eradicate it, for it thrives in the soil of pride and fear. Yet, there is a force more potent than any human strategy—**love**. Not the sentimental love of fleeting emotions, but *agape (A Greek word for unconditional love)*: the selfless, sacrificial, and transformative love of Yah.

This divine love, exemplified in Christ, is the only antidote to the poison of racial division. It tears down walls, heals ancient wounds, and unites what sin has torn apart. As we turn to Scripture, we find that love is not merely a virtue but the very heartbeat of God's redemptive plan for humanity.

This kind of love is not natural to humanity. It is divine. It is the love that sent Yahusha (Jesus) to the cross. It is the love that reaches out to sinners, outcasts, and enemies. It is the love that turned Saul, the persecutor, into Paul, the apostle. And it is the love that has the power to dissolve racial prejudice, heal generational wounds, and unify mankind under one Creator.

The Apostle Paul's words in 1 Corinthians 13 cut to the core of the matter:

"If I speak in the tongues of men or of angels but do not have love, I am only a resounding gong or a clanging cymbal... Love is patient; love is kind. It does not envy, it does not boast, it is not proud. It does not dishonor others, it is not self-seeking, it is not easily angered, it keeps no record of wrongs..."

Here, Paul dismantles the illusion that any effort—even justice-driven activism—holds no meaning without love. Racial reconciliation devoid of love becomes performative, a "clanging cymbal" of empty gestures.

True love, as defined by God, is active: it listens without defensiveness, forgives without conditions, and sees the divine image in every soul.

In Ephesians 2:14–18, Paul declares that Christ *"Himself is our peace, who has made the two groups one and has destroyed the barrier, the dividing wall of hostility."* The cross abolishes the enmity between Jews and Gentiles, a metaphor for all racial divides. This unity is not assimilation but a celebration of diversity under the banner of Christ's lordship. The principle applies to all racial and ethnic divisions.

Yahusha came to break down barriers—not just between God and man, but between man and man.

Consider the Samaritan woman at the well (John 4). Yahusha broke multiple cultural barriers when speaking to her—she was a Samaritan, a woman, and an outcast. Yet, He did not see her as an "other." He saw her as a person in need of truth and redemption. His love was not hindered by race, gender, or social standing.

If we claim to follow Him, can we love any differently?

Love in Action

It is not enough to talk about love. It must be lived.

1. Forgiveness: Liberating the Heart

Forgiveness is love's first radical act. It does not excuse injustice but releases its grip on our souls.

Love means releasing bitterness and choosing grace. Forgiveness is not ignoring the pain of racism but refusing to let it define us. It is the way forward.

I recall a conversation with Marcus, a man who spent 15 years imprisoned under racially biased sentencing. When he spoke of forgiving the judge who condemned him, I asked, "How?" He replied, "Bitterness was my second prison. Christ taught me to surrender the keys."

Forgiveness breaks generational cycles of retaliation, creating space for healing.

2. Understanding: The Ministry of Listening

Love demands empathy—entering another's story without an agenda.

At Bridge Builders Newark, we hosted "Dinner Dialogues," where Black, white, and Latino coworkers shared meals and personal histories. One evening, a white contractor tearfully confessed his family's legacy of segregationist policies. A Black colleague responded, "Your honesty is a bridge. Let's cross it together."

Understanding begins when we listen to learn, not to rebut. Love listens. It seeks to understand the experiences and perspectives of others rather than dismissing or minimizing their pain. It values the truth of their story.

3. Breaking Generational Cycles: Intentional Legacy

Love is proactive. Love is generational. The biases and prejudices passed down through families and cultures can end with those who choose love over hate. Love challenges inherited mindsets and replaces them with the truth of Yah.

My wife, Cheryl, and I taught our family and the congregation we Pastor to reject the "us vs. them" narratives we inherited. We have been blessed to understand for many years that "They" are not to blame or hold resentment towards. Rather, rejoice in who you are created to be and judge every person based on their own merit. Never lump everyone into general categories based on ignorance or even negative, personal interactions with a few. Individuals are never representative of entire people groups.

Becoming Love's Ambassadors

Racism cannot be legislated away. It cannot be debated out of existence. It cannot be silenced by force. It can only be overcome by love. Love is not passive; it is a verb. It is an active force that heals the deepest divides. Let us choose to love as He first loved us. To dismantle racism, we must:

- Pray Boldly: Ask God to reveal hidden biases and heal communal wounds.

- Step into Discomfort: Attend a worship service, community event, or meal in a culture different from your own.

- Invest Relationally: Mentor, hire or collaborate

across racial lines. At Bridge Builders, our "mixed-race" teams model unity daily.

- Advocate Justly: Challenge policies that marginalize but do so with grace, not vitriol.

The Tapestry of Unity

In Revelation 7:9, John envisions a multitude "from every nation, tribe, people, and language" worshiping together. This is love's ultimate triumph—a mosaic of redeemed humanity. Until that day, we are called to weave threads of love into the fractured fabric of our world.

Racial prejudice thrives where love is absent. But love—God's love—casts out fear (1 John 4:18). It is not a fleeting emotion but a revolution. As we embody it, we become living proof that the myth of race cannot withstand the power of truth.

Through forgiveness, understanding, and intentional reconciliation, divine love dismantles racism's strongholds and forges a path to unity.

"Above all, love each other deeply because love covers over a multitude of sins."—1 Peter 4:8.

Chapter 14: Living as One in Christ

The world insists on defining us by race, ethnicity, or nationality—categories that fissure humanity into fragments. But Scripture offers a radical alternative: *"There is neither Jew nor Gentile, neither slave nor free, nor is there male and female, for you are all one in Christ Jesus"* (Galatians 3:28).

This is not wishful thinking; it is a divine decree. To live as one in Christ is to step into a kingdom reality where earthly labels dissolve, and our shared identity as God's children takes precedence.

This chapter is a call to embrace that truth, reject division, and become living testimonies of unity in a splintered world.

1. Embracing Our Spiritual Identity

Christ's death and resurrection did more than secure individual salvation—it forged a new humanity.

When Paul declares, "You have put off the old self with its practices and have put on the new self, which is being renewed in knowledge in the image of its Creator" (Colossians 3:9–10), he invites us to shed the "old self" of racial pride, prejudice, and tribalism.

Our primary identity is no longer rooted in skin color, culture, or lineage but in Christ's redemptive work.

My former Pastor tells the story of a vision from the

Lord that struck him so heavily that his whole ministry was shaped by it. He recounts the day that he was in a supermarket shopping, and while standing in line, he surveyed all of the different types of people groups represented in the store and asked himself, "Why can't my church be like this?" Today, 30 years later, he has one of the most diverse churches I know of – it can be done!

2. Practical Steps for Living as Reconcilers

- See Others Through God's Eyes

Racial bias thrives when we view people as categories rather than individuals. Jesus modeled a different approach: He saw Zacchaeus not as a "greedy tax collector" but as a son of Abraham (Luke 19:1–9). To see others through God's eyes means:

Pray for spiritual sight: Ask God to reveal His love for every person you encounter.

Challenge stereotypes: Replace assumptions with curiosity. "What is their story? How has God shaped them?"

Celebrate diversity: The Body of Christ is meant to be multiethnic (Revelation 7:9). Diversity reflects God's creativity, not division.

- Reject Divisive Language and Mindsets

Words have power. The tongue can "spark a forest fire" of strife (James 3:5–6). Use words to reject division:

Avoid racialized labels: Terms like "those people" or "your kind", which dehumanize. Speak of individuals, not groups.

Reframe narratives: When a friend lamented, "Black and white folks will never get along," I countered, "But what if we're family? Families fight, but they also forgive."

Silence gossip: Refuse to entertain prejudiced jokes or stereotypes, even in private.

- Lead by Example in Key Spheres

Families: Teach children to honor all people as image-bearers. A friend of mine's daughter once asked why her friend's skin was darker. My friend replied, "God painted us different colors to show His artistry. Isn't it beautiful?"

Workplaces: Advocate for equity. At Bridge Builders Newark, we prioritize hiring formerly incarcerated individuals and offering mentorship alongside employment. One client confessed, "I used to judge these men. Now I see their potential."

Churches: The words of one of the most famous leaders for human and civil rights once said that the most segregated time in America is 11:00 on Sunday morning (which is the traditional meeting time for most churches in the US). These words still ring true today. However, it's okay to have fellowship with people of the same cultural identity. The problem is when we put up prejudicial barriers to engagement with others, all while claiming to live in the Love of Yahweh. This, too, is also error, vanity, and vexation of the spirit – to borrow a phrase from Solomon (Ecclesiates). May we drop our barriers and prejudices and proceed towards a better world – it can be done!

3. Overcoming Prejudice through Faith

In the 1990s, a retired police officer who had once enforced segregationist policies. Haunted by guilt, he avoided Black communities for years. During a Bible study on Matthew 5:23–24 (*"If you are offering your gift at the altar and remember your brother has something against you…"*), he broke down. He spent months apologizing to those he'd wronged, even joining our ministry's outreach in Newark. "I thought I was too broken to change," he said. "But grace is stronger than hate."

Prejudice cannot survive an intentional relationship. Jesus ate with sinners, touched lepers, and honored Samaritans. Likewise, we must:

- Seek uncomfortable friendships: Dine with someone of another ethnicity. Attend a cultural celebration.

- Listen without defense: When a Black congregant shared her fears of racial profiling, a white church member initially argued, "Not all cops—" until he paused and said, "Help me understand."

- Repent publicly: A business leader once confessed to our team, "I've excluded qualified candidates because of bias. Forgive me." His humility sparked a company-wide equity audit.

4. The Ripple Effect of Unity

A father once taught his son: "You don't have to agree to respect. But in Christ, you can do more—you can love." Decades later, that son watched his kid, now a teacher, mediate a conflict between students of rival gangs.

"You're not Crip or Blood here," he told them. "You're my students. Act like it." Over time, their hostility softened into mutual aid. Kingdom identity outlasts earthly divisions.

Ambassadors of a New Reality

Living as one in Christ is not a passive ideal—it is a daily rebellion against the world's divisions. It requires us to *"clothe ourselves with compassion, kindness, humility, gentleness, and patience"* (Colossians 3:12), armor that deflects prejudice and radiates grace.

The church is called to be a preview of Revelation 7:9—a people unified not by uniformity but by shared redemption. As we model this, we offer a weary world more than rhetoric; we offer proof that the myth of race collapses before the power of Christ.

Spiritual transformation enables believers to model unity and reconciliation in a divided world. By seeing others through God's eyes, rejecting divisive mindsets, and leading with Christ-like love, we become living testimonies of a kingdom where racial barriers cannot stand.

"For He Himself is our peace, who has made the two groups one and has destroyed the barrier, the dividing wall of hostility." —Ephesians 2:14.

Chapter 15: A Call To Action

In these pages, we have covered a lot of ground in terms of history, experience, theology, and truth telling. However, it's time to go beyond comprehension. Knowledge is not where the journey ends; rather, it starts with how we use it. Recognizing that the idea of race as a fallacy useless if we do not take concrete steps to dispel it. What good is truth if it never finds its way to our hearts, families, and our communities?

This is not just a concluding chapter. It is an invitation. A call.

You are already aware that race, as we have come to understand it, does not exist if you have read this far. Race was constructed, word for word, lie for lie, and piece by piece. Despite this, the world has been influenced by this untruth for millennia. It has created invisible barriers that persist in our communities to this day, rewritten history, shattered families, and dictated policy. However, those walls are not impenetrable if race is a myth. They could be destroyed.

First, we reject the labels not only in theory but also in our daily thoughts, words, and guidance of the next generation. This calls for having the guts to question the lighthearted remarks, the strongly held presumptions, and the jokes that pass for innocuous. It entails deciding every day to turn away from things that strengthen division and toward things that foster unity.

However, this goes beyond simply exposing lies. It's

about accepting reality. We weren't valued according to our pigment or closeness to power; rather, we were made in Yah's image. Our value stems from something much more profound than our background or social standing. Identity starts there—not in appearance, but in heart. In divine intention, not in the shackles of history.

We have been conditioned by the world to distinguish between us and them, superior and inferior, domestic and alien. However, the truth tells us that we are all part of the same creation. Culture, language, geography, and experience are all different, yet they are never fundamentally different. And, never worth erecting barriers because of them. The racial lie starts to fall apart before our very eyes the more we start to view people the way Yah does.

It will take bravery to live this truth. Sometimes, following the crowd seems more comfortable than standing up for what's right, and the old habits will feel more natural. However, we are not meant for comfort. Furthermore, when truth is acted upon, it changes systems as well as hearts. Communities are reshaped by it. Hardened minds are softened by it. Additionally, it heals areas where division used to be the norm.

It begins with the little things: our speech, our listening, and our correction. The next generation watches what we approve of and what we disapprove of at the dinner table. It takes place in our neighborhoods, places of employment, and places of worship, where we get to live out what it means to walk in love and truth.

Additionally, we must keep in mind that this job is not about guilt. Shame isn't the issue. Staying mired in the past or counting wrongs is not the point. This has to do with accountability. The sort of accountability that declares, "Even though I did not cause the issue, I am dedicated to contributing to its resolution." Freedom comes from this duty, not only for ourselves but also for everyone around us.

Community transformation follows personal transformation. However, this isn't always the case. Hearts can remain unaffected by changes in systems. However, everything surrounding a changing heart must also adapt. This revolution starts with the quiet determination of an individual who chooses to live a different life, not led by legislation or news headlines.

Throughout this book, we have discussed love—not as a gentle ideal but as a power capable of reversing centuries of conflict. This is the kind of love that inspires us to take action, disrupts generational cycles, and restores what hatred has destroyed. This love is not a feeling that is passive. It's a discipline. A decision. And it's the only path to success.

Truth is a good place to start if you're unsure where to begin. Give it time to sink in. Allow it to take the place of all inherited lies. Allow it to influence your thoughts, speech, and mannerisms. Then, allow compassion to blossom from that truth and action to follow from that compassion.

This is a call to those who are prepared to live in the light and are sick of the falsehood. This appeals to people who have witnessed the divide and have the audacity to think that togetherness is still achievable. An exhortation to you, the reader, to fulfill your destiny as a truth-teller, peacemaker, and reconciler rather than as a passive observer.

The damage caused by the myth of race is sufficient.

However, what is the reality? The ability to deconstruct lies and rebuild in the truth.

Consider yourself officially invited. Let's Go!!